The Runaway Heart

And Other Tales

Also by Hermann Stehr from K A Nitz:

The Engraver

Meicke, the Devil

The Shingle Maker and Other Tales

Leonore Griebel

The Buried God

The Shimmer of the Assistant and Other Tales

The Twilight and Other Tales

Three Nights

Stories from the Mandel House

The Runaway Heart
And Other Tales

Hermann Stehr

K A Nitz

WELLINGTON

Dates of first publication in German:
Das entlaufene Herz 1913
Wendelin Heinelt 1909
Das Feuer 1919
Das Gotschdorfer Weib 1916
Der Feuersamen 1907

ISBN: 978-0-473-28163-2

Contents

The Runaway Heart..................7

Wendelin Heinelt..................59

The Fire...................103

The Gotschdorf Woman.......109

The Fire Seeds.....................129

The Runaway Heart

Hermann Stehr

1

Whenever the music ends in villages, the
moon draws back a bit, hangs a veil over
its white face, closes its shadowy eyes, and turns
the young people adrift. For it knows they will
then all carry such a bright fiery light in themselves that it cannot rise against it with its pale
light.

On such a night, the heart on earth whose tale
I will now tell came alive.

The tavern "of the three stalks" lay in a high
raised area which sank on all sides towards the
mountains on which three villages flowed up
three valleys, so high up that the last houses
hung completely above the forest: Klein-Pinz,
Groß-Mohrau and Wenig-Rohme.

They all lay quiet and faded for week after
week in the forest and above the fields, and of
the three villages, Klein-Pinz was the most in-
conspicuous. The houses of which it consisted
had few furrows of their own and if the stream,
which fell day and night with a whisper over little
rocky steps into a pond, had not been in its
midst, the people of this tiny little village would
have languished and died in their lonely poverty.
But the whispering of the water kept them alive,

and the young men were jaunty and agile and the girls fresh and bright-eyed like the ripples of water running past them.

Hard by the waterfall of Klein-Pinz stood the house of Lenore Negwer. It had been moved so close to the drop that, in adverse winds, the drops of the falling stream sprayed onto its panes and the roar filled the house without break so that there was no peace at all for a single thought.

Thus for this house things went both better and worse than for all the other houses of Klein-Pinz. Better, for it needed to deal with nothing else, worse, because it had nothing else in the world.

Within living memory, only mothers had lived in it, that is, those who never knew in what way they had come to have a child. God liked to shepherd as he wanted, there was nothing to be done about it. Hardly did the little breasts press through the jacket of a Negwer girl than the roaring in the house became so strong that it led the maiden out, and when she returned, she was doubled. It proved thus for Lenore Negwer, her mother had to suffer the same fate and her grandmother had been played with in the same way. Of more remote ancestors, nobody could think anymore; but it had surely been no different with them.

When the difficult hour approached for the poor being, it was decided that no man should ever come near her again, and as certainly as the hot roar in the maelstrom had turned her, as firmly did each hold to the resolution all the way to their lonely death.

They did not bring more than one child into the world, and it was always a girl.

The house was thus called by everyone that of "the water maidens", and some really believed that something not right was going on there. It was said that the Negwer girls only had to sit by the water in the light of the moon for it to happen. But those about which this was spoken did not say "yes" or "no" to it; were surely sad in the first weeks with their fatherless child, but gathered themselves in the quiet, cheerful way which had formed their inheritance from time immemorial, bent down diligently in the few furrows behind their house, collected wood in the forest, carried mushrooms and berries to the town and smiled peacefully when they saw other women suffering under their husbands.

Soon they had forgotten entirely from whom they had received their girl, and if they wandered with their thoughts back into their life, they came to a colourful, roaring gate under which they had lain in jubilation, and were free of every ache. Their hair remained blond even in old age, their eyes kept their brilliance, and when creases were already running through the faces of others, their cheeks still bloomed maidenly smooth.

The daughter of Lenore Negwer was called Melanie.

With her the story begins.

She was taller and more beautiful than her maternal forebears before her. Her blue eyes carried in their depths a bronze light, and everyone she looked at was overcome by a soft rapture, if it was a young man; when an older man peered into them, he had to turn around and slap his thigh in astonishment. Thus she was at sixteen years, and Melanie did not know anything yet about men, but was only annoyed that the young men stared after her. But sometimes, when she was sitting alone in the living room and listening to the roar of the water through the window, it sounded to her as if a thousand little musicians were skipping singing and fiddling in confusion. It droned humming under the large stones so that it became wondrously anxious in her breast, and when she bent out to look at what was actually happening, she looked into a colourful peacock's crescent which floated up and down in the light over the water as if it were stirred by a mysterious draught. Then such a sunny mist came over her that she had to sink back quite faint and powerless, and sit there for a long time yet with a face as if she were falling into a nameless daydream.

Then her mother knew that the hot roaring was close to the girl and was around her day and night. In the field, Melanie's hoe had to ring by her own; with berry picking, she did not let the red headscarf out of her eyes; at dusk she always stood behind her; and even in the night, she did not leave her side. For what everyone who had become a mother in the house by the waterfall had wanted, Lenore Negwer also strove for: her girl would not submit to the fate of the water maidens, but be led like others on the path through the fate of marriage into life, and not founder like her mother and grandmother in the fiery whirl of a premature wedding night. For that reason, she guarded Melanie like her own eyes, and when the girl's look was some days in far too deep a blaze, she knew how to frighten the child with all sorts of gruesome stories so that the girl agreed to go lie in bed in her clothes. Her mother rested likewise next to Melanie on the bed and had in addition bound her daughter's arm to her wrist with an apron string.

Only no apple that is ripe remains hanging on the tree, and if nobody shakes it, it falls by itself to the ground. On a summer Sunday's night, Melanie's hour had come. She had already been groggy the whole day. Everything she grasped fell from her hands. When an unexpected noise arose next to her, she started with a little squeal, and when she had been looking for a long time into the light which was flickering over the field, she felt the waves of the light entering her body and becoming so strong there that she would have liked most of all to run out, and would have twirled in the solitary field with exultant singing until she fell over breathless.

When she now lay in the night and listened to the falling stream, the sound of the waves sounded beautiful, like nothing she had ever heard before. The water was again singing all that it had absorbed during the day on its course through the forest, the fields and the village: the jubilation of the birdsong, the soft swishing of the grass and the grain, the cry of the young men and their laughter, the singing of the girls who had been strolling by it. The entire life of the day sounded in the fall of the water, but more enraptured still, more enticing, more furtive, sweeter. The girl listened thus to the music so that she was quite intoxicated. Her pulse was hammering so that her entire body shook, and she had to push the covers down with her free arm because it seemed to be filled with smouldering coals instead of feathers; she finally said to her mother softly, "Don't you hear how the water is singing?" But she did not answer, for she was already asleep and travelling over all the mountains in her dream. Then the girl raised her head a little and looked up to the window. The moonlight was playing on the leaves of the bushes so that they glistened like silver coins.

As Melanie lost herself in this play of light for a little while, something magically incomprehensible happened. A mysterious wind passed into the singing roar and led it away. It was carried away from the house, softer and ever softer, and expired completely in a nocturnal silence that was unbearable. The countless little hammers in her body stopped beating, her breast seemed nailed down and threatening to burst. So as not to die, she carefully slipped the apron string from her arm, squirmed noiselessly out of the bed, cast off her dress in front of the wardrobe, adorned herself quickly with the best things she had, and left the house. As she stepped into the field, she heard the exulting, fiddling, and singing of the water already far beyond the village, drawing enticingly into the night. She hitched up her dress and sprang after it as quickly as her legs could carry her. She thus left the village. For some time, she thought she had lost the resounding roar. But when she arrived up on the plateau, she saw the tavern of the three stalks standing with its brightly lit windows like a carousel and heard it blaring a music into the night entirely as if the exulting roar of the waterfall had been carried by the wind into the tavern, and it enticed with a thousand mysterious voices like it had infatuated her so often at the window in her mother's room. She forgot her mother and the apron string and soon stood up by the entrance to the saloon. Hardly had a young man seen her appear in the doorway, than he swerved on the way to his dance partner, took Melanie by the arm and whirled with her through the saloon so that it seemed to her as if she were being carried in jubilation through the air.

Thus the long hours of the night passed.

The shadow dials of the solitary trees in the fields extended further and further. It finally irritated the moon to count the heartbeats of lonely time, and he sank down wearily, ever nearer towards the long mountain wall which leaned out like a giant, dark saw with teeth turned upwards into the heavens. It was already smouldering a yellowy white on the tips of the forest's trees. But then it seemed to give a jerk and stop its rolling down. For the tavern of the three stalks was just whinnying its last three jubilant closing fanfares. The shadows of the dancers were thrown across the windows once more in a whirling rush, then the music broke off as if someone had shattered a violin against the wall. The light in the windows was extinguished and the night clambered blackly into the empty hatches. In the wide door, the couples thronged, joking around and laughing, and dispersed along the paths and field margins across the plateau.

The moon squinted once more with an ill-tempered glare from its surly face, as if it wanted to say to those wandering home, "It was about time that you went. I could not have stayed up here in the sky any longer. For the morning is already burning my back." Then it pulled together a few cloths of mist which lay over the forest, drew them over its pane and began to sleep.

But the young men and women who had been brought together by the music, when they saw that the moon was darkening, pressed together closer and closer. They exchanged their breath under kisses and entangled themselves in this way. The paths and field margins sank in front of them, the fields looked like palely gleaming waves about to swim away. The trees swayed in the fields. The stars trembled as though drunk in the heavens, the entire earth revolved like a board driven on a current.

Melanie, who was sampling such a thing for the first time, became so weak about her heart that she had to sit down under a tall willow tree which stood on the corner of a large field of oats. Now the heavens lay above her, and when she looked up, she did not know if she were looking into the eyes of the man by her, or in the eyes of the stars, and she could not distinguish whether the mysterious, lulling music of the air was talking to her or the mouth of a man. Her blood got caught, the whole world became a fiery gate under which she lay, and her heart was drawing her ever deeper into the fiery whirl.

Then at the last moment, a bird shot out from the stalks next to her and rushed with a shrill cry of fright into the heavens. That brought Melanie to her senses. She pulled her overflooding heart back and opened her eyes in fright. Then she saw above her a pale, distorted man's face, whose lips stammered and who had the eyes of a mad beast.

With a scream, shrill as a bird's, she sprang up, pushed the man back with a shove against his chest, and rushed away in mad flight. Her mother was meanwhile sitting full of anguish in her bed and waiting. She finally heard her daughter gasping, running against the door, and collapsing. And when Lenore opened the door, she saw Melanie lying on the threshold as though lifeless. Her hair was unfastened and hanging raggedly over her pale face. Her dress was open and her fingers were pressed into her young breasts protectively. The tears entered her mother's eyes. She sat down next to Melanie on the threshold and looked at her. "After all, after all," Lenore murmured in despair. Then she gathered up the unconscious girl and carried her in to bed.

2

Lenore Negwer thought, and nothing else seemed possible, that her daughter had submitted to the fate of the house.

Thus she put Melanie into her own bed, carried the girl's bed into the living room, prepared breakfast, placed it on the table, searched for the stick and the cloth for mushroom collecting and said, already halfway through the doorway, the doorhandle in her hand, "When you are then up to it, there is something standing there ready to eat," then threw a half glance of anguish and rancour at the collapsed girl, and left the house without closing the door.

For she was angry with her girl, but more from love, that she had caused her and herself such anguish, and not avoided her mother's anguish. So she went into the forest and did not want to return again until all the anger and rancour had left her. She ate the bread that she had wrapped up, plucked some berries, and when her throat became dry, she drank a handful of water from one of the many rivulets which tinkled everywhere through the forest. At night she slept in the fodder rack left for wild animals, which was still full of winter hay. She certainly needed little sustenance on the first day and little sleep on the first night. Only, the humming of the tree tops slowly sounded brighter and higher, the water played ever more happily through the forest, and when she awoke on the third morning, it seemed to her as if someone were waving a coloured cloth through the air over her and tittering so cheerfully at the same time that it sounded as if the entire forest were laughing at her.

Then Lenore climbed out from the stalks of her bed, brushed back her hair and said to herself, "Certainly, I won't stay in the forest for ever."

Then she set off again on the search for mushrooms and had nothing to object to when she noticed that it led further and further towards Klein-Pinz. In the evening, she saw the village's first houses through the trees. But she sat down and waited until she could no longer discern the rooves in the darkness. 'For', she thought to herself, 'if I come too early, the girl will probably think that what she has done is not so bad and will load up a new mob at the first opportunity.'

She would perhaps have spun the thought a few steps further into tartness, but at the first house, the back door facing the forest now opened and a young mother with a little, blond haired shirt-puller on her arm came into the light of an open lamp above the threshold so that it looked as if the Blessed Mother herself with the little Jesus was approaching Lenore Negwer out of the darkness of the world; and the woman, who had just then been making her teeth numb with vinegar, felt such a blissful blow to her chest that she threw her load of mushrooms on her back and set off homewards without turning around.

Below the front door, a man was running towards her who tried to spring past her and would have almost knocked her over. "Hey!", she said, "I'm still here!", turned around and looked to see where the young man was running to. If he had gone off towards Groß-Mohrau, everything would have been made easier.

But the young man's shadow shot straight through under the plum trees and vanished into the field.

"You could at least have shut the gate," Lenore murmured angrily, closed the gate behind her, crossed the narrow hallway, stepping loudly, and opened the door to the living room and called her daughter's name.

She had expected that the girl would emerge out of a corner, putting her clothes to right and approaching her.

Nobody stirred. Nobody answered.

'She is ashamed, the poor thing,' Lenore thought and said kindheartedly, "Just be good, Melanie, and light a little candle."

Still not a sound stirred.

Then the quiet fear ran through the woman like a cold drop of water down her back. She groped around agitatedly on the bench by the stove for the matches, and when she found none, she ran to the stairs up to the loft and screamed fearfully, "Melanie!"

All she heard above was the cat jumping down from something, a sound like a rubber ball falling to the ground.

Then everything was still again like in the middle of a stone. Even when Lenore lit the lamp and searched through room after room with the light, even the cellar in the end, she did not find her daughter. Stepping outside and affectionately clucking into the night was just as in vain.

And when the poor woman had combed through the little house from top to bottom again, she always returned to the open, ransacked wardrobe, counted Melanie's shoes and shirts and said apprehensively, "The stupid girl would not have run away?!"

When she had thought that to herself for the third, fourth time, the water of the falls outside began suddenly to churn, as if it were not tossing waves, but stones through an iron sieve into the pool. It was a crashing that shook the windows. Then Lenore sank onto the bench and began to cry, for now she knew it could be nothing else: Melanie had gone away and done something to herself. And the poor woman cried until the agitations of her sorrow were lost in the restive boulders of grey dreams. On awakening she was still sitting on the bench at the window and Melanie was not there.

Only the morning hung brightly from the roof. The sun was playing on the pool, and a little mist, white, hazy and glistening like a bride's veil, lay over the peaceful mirrored surface of the water, trembling sometimes as though from a sudden breath, then rising wavering, stretched, and dispersing in the light.

Then her thoughts became easier and lighter, she had the courage to remember her own life, the time when she had been thrown to the ground by the fiery jolt so that it had made her blind and she had roamed about for days in the forest. It had befallen her mother similarly, and when exhaustion came over Melanie or the intoxication was stilled, then the way home would run by itself under her feet and she would suddenly unlatch the door one day.

That reassured Lenore completely.

She dragged the old cradle out from behind the junk in the attic and dusted it off; fetched the little smocks out from the depths of the chest and laid them in the drawer of the commode. Then she opened her heart quite wide in forgiving love and thought, 'Melanie must notice it, wherever she is, and even if just as a shimmer glowing from afar into her darkness.'

3

But Lenore Negwer waited in vain for her daughter. For Melanie's eyes had opened in good time to that image to which the fears of each of her maternal forebears had contributed something.

The vision had always first come over her maternal forebears after they had played for their fortune in the shadow of the man and lost everything. For the last Negwer girl, it had raised her eyelids before it could carry her into the sightless.

She had probably arisen like all her maternal forebears from the branch of this maternal house as a blazing bud, but, in bursting, the blossom petals had suddenly, as though by a miracle, coloured her soul white, and her shirt was as cool as if it had never been bleached by the sun but only in the moonlight. This turn of fate had passed behind the corner as it were like a storm so that her consciousness of it had been blown away.

She had not felt her mother lift her from the threshold and carry her to bed, she knew nothing of the angry look which had mixed rancour and anguish, nor even Lenore's loveless words of parting. But when she rose after a long time and could look around, she discovered the half loaf of bread, the bowl full of milk and the butter dish and knew that her mother had gone away in anger because she had thought she had come home with a torn veil.

Then the girl drew her knees up, buried her face in her hands and said, "It happened to me for sure!" The tears fell slowly from her eyes like raindrops falling from drooping leaves. She cried and cried and did not notice that the day was coming to an end and the evening arriving. In the end, her eyes were dry and glowing like a lead ball which has lain the whole day in the heat, and when she looked up, the night was already sitting darkly around the waterfall and counting loud and distinctly every little wave, and the meagre light of the rising moon was lighting up the underside of the leaves of the bushes as if someone with a little lantern were standing on the ground and shining it up into the branches.

The longer Melanie looked into the shimmering bushes, the more beyond doubt it became for her that someone was standing there in the bushes under her window and shining a light upwards. But before she convinced herself whether her suspicion was warranted, she climbed from the bed to close the front door. She had become groggy from the long time thinking, the walls of the hallway swayed as if they were seething in the darkness, and even when she had returned to the living room again, the window was running like two grey cats chasing each other through the darkness, and Melanie grasped her breast to free herself from a pressure. Then the girl noticed that her bust was still uncovered and when she touched her body, it seemed at once to her as if she were applying strange hands to herself, and the same terror, the same roaring ran through her body as it had in the previous night in the field when the man's eyes were above her.

"If now for anything, someone were to be standing under the window," she pondered shaking and closed her dress with trembling hands. It was beating in her as if someone were trying to free themselves with impassioned fists. She had to close her eyes, the convulsions of her heart seized her so, and when she raised her eyelids again, she had, without knowing it, moved to the window, propped herself with stiff arms on the window sill and looked out. At the same time, she was struggling for air because her breath was being torn from her breast as though with hot shovels. She leant thus for a long while without consciousness of herself and pressed her burning forehead onto the cold pane until the mist before her face finally lightened more and more and she saw the leaves touching gently again and heard the water falling muffled over the stones. But when she opened the window to see what had actually frightened her, a man really did stand by the wall, raising his arms to her and beseeching her with a stammer from his pale face to let him in or to come out to him. His eyes looked in the night like those of a mad, drunken beast.

Melanie was overwhelmed by horror again. She slammed the window shut so that the panes rattled and ran through the room, across to the hallway, for she recalled that she had only latched the front door. But the young man outside had probably noted that Melanie was alone. For when the girl sprang away from the window, he also left his place by the wall and ran around the house so as to yet reach the door before his coveted one. He ran with great strides so that you could hear the stones clattering under his feet.

But Melanie beat the ardent man to it. As she tore the bolt across, the man flew with a crash against the door so that the rusty hinges creaked, and then attempted through all sorts of violence to gain mastery over the door. But his lifting and pushing and rattling were of no use. In between, he whispered through the crack that he would kill himself if she did not let him in, that he wanted nothing else but to speak with her, that he loved her and had serious intentions; knocked now and then for variety sometimes on one, sometimes on the other window, and supposedly went away in the end with imprecations. Only he returned after a long time and, with a racket against the door, began the series of all his mad and gentle siege techniques anew.

Melanie must have been on her legs for hours. For when she lay down quietly and let the soft imprecations of the lover work on her, she felt herself becoming without as though sleepwalking and had to press against her heart primly with her fists because it was drawing her with fervent ribbons sometimes to the window, sometimes to the door. When the young man finally eased up and his steps tailed off loudly and ill-temperedly into the night, Melanie was exhausted. In the end, she felt so battered in mood and absolutely wretched that she began quietly crying again.

4

Melanie had been so startled within by the new fear that she slept deeply, almost as though lifelessly, and when she opened her eyes in the grey morning of the next day, her soul could not find its way back out of the expanse straightaway.

But when she had sunk through the last inner courtyards of her dream into the day, the memory of the hustling of the previous evening ambushed her, and she was torn from the wavering grandeur into the midst of a dark engine. She realised that if she remained any longer in her mother's house, then her blind, ardently hungry heart would never be subdued, but instead one day she would close her eyes, and when she freed her sight again, she would then find herself again in the place where all her maternal forebears had spent their lives, on the side namely where the wind of fate plays with nothing but the bonnet ribbons of old maids, the coattails of old bachelors, and the cloths covering the beggars' baskets.

"Who knows when my mother will come back, and if she just stays away for a day and a night, I will perhaps have already weakened and have let myself be covered by the man."

Melanie pondered all that the way young people ponder who are having their first real anguish in life, in such a fervour that she just flew around and roamed restlessly about the entire house, and she always thought she heard steps creeping up behind her, and discerned the stifled breath of the lurker from the corners. She ran back into the living room in the end and said despondently, her entire body shaking, "I must not stay another hour in my mother's house," put her weekday clothes on, packed her Sunday things in a freshly washed carryall, like those which village people tend to carry on their backs, drank the rest of the milk, ate a small sandwich, and placed the remaining bread with her belongings. Then she sat down on the bench by the window and looked tensely at the path which passed by the bushes on the other side of the waterfall.

She was not sitting for too long, when she heard a wagon creaking up the Klein-Pinz path from the mountains; and again, not long after, the haggard head of an old, fox-red horse moved past, sunken with stoicism and age, slowly and circuitously, and a wooden wagon was dragging behind, on which old Gruner, the Pinz errand wagoner, crouched as ever, like a hen after the last evening crow, his head drawn into his coat as if into puffed up feathers.

Melanie quickly gathered up the carryall from the bench, sprang to her feet, and hurried out of the house. On the threshold, she kissed the left and right door posts, devotedly and apprehensively, like the two cheeks of a dear face, and apologised in thought to her mother for all the sorrow which she had forced her to prepare for. Then she hurried behind the house down the steep path through the plum trees to the end of the village, felt herself crying, but did not stop for that, instead wiping away the tears with the forefinger of her free hand whilst running, and shaking them off next to herself onto the grass.

Below the village, behind Zucker's mill where the path prepared with a long arc to clamber up the slope to the plateau, she met up with old Gruner's wagon, which was rolling on more hurriedly and with the drawbar of the fox pushing up the yoke onto the neck because the road had to overcome a small dip before its climb. The old horse almost had to act as if someone knew about it, although it jerked like on a summer jaunt, and Gruner had to take a firmer hold with the reins so that it did not stumble over its own legs. Thus the wagon creaked onward as if it really wanted to go past in flight, pushing the backrests up.

Melanie had taken the carryall from her back and, because she could not make herself understood any other way, raised the large, white pack into the air as a sign that she wanted a lift. The old man nodded, but was driven on by the self-willed rush of the wagon complete with its horse and did not stop until it was behind the pool at the foot of the hill.

"A mad, old wench," Gruner said and looked back at Melanie approaching hurriedly. "Right, little Mel, that's what I call running! Yes, yes, here around the pond, the old calf of the fox always acts confused. Where are you going then?"

"To the town," the girl suggested timidly.

"Yes, with mushrooms or something, eh?" he asked further.

Melanie nodded ambiguously and prepared to climb up.

"Shall I give you a little push from behind?" Gruner joked, and when he saw that Melanie was seated, he cracked the whip, crawled back into his coat and dozed again in the sluggish gait of his horse and the gentle clatter of his wagon.

When they finally arrived on the humped plateau and were in sight of the tavern of the three stalks, it quietly passed over Melanie. She saw a flickering light steaming from the ground, and by the oat field at whose corner the willow climbed up high into the air, such a heat struck her in the breast that she lowered her eyes and had to stuff around in her carryall because she thought old Gruner was looking at her with mocking eyes.

'If only he doesn't stop at the tavern!' Melanie wrestled within almost beseechingly. She heard the wheels creak louder as though thrown back by a wall, and then the broad shadow of the building also fell over her. Now the landlord would step out from the door and look at her.

Melanie felt her face burning like it was on fire and did not dare to look up.

But, thank God, Gruner pulled the fox back from rushing to the fodder rack and drove it quickly past with an irritated crack of his whip. The girl let her eyes happily close and listened through the soft sounds of the wheels so that the tavern was like a gentle humming in the fields, remained gentler and ever gentler behind her, and finally fell silent.

After that Melanie dared to open her eyes and was astonished at the sort of transformation which had taken place in the world, for heaven and earth stood like a colourful and festive gate around her, a gate into which she was passing.

The fields billowed in a silvery light, bushes often moved past close to the wagon. The familiar surroundings seemed foreign to the girl, distant as if blissfully enchanted.

Thus they travelled through Totchendorf, then through Heinrichau, and the further they went, the deeper Melanie was carried into a great liberation and did not think anymore of what had driven her away, until the Riedersbach town hall's tower appeared out of the fields, at first like the helmet spike of a gendarme riding up, then growing into the thin top of a fir tree, and soon rising up already with the small arched windows into the smoky blue, and the first house rooves were thronging in a jumble under it.

Then Melanie was reminded of what she actually wanted from her journey into the world. She had to now make a decision, and as is the habit of early youth, she turned her thoughts to the most distant, deepest urge of her soul and came to the conviction that she could not return to her mother's house before she had found a husband who did not have the beast flickering in his eyes when he looked at her. After the girl had thought that, a fine, high glow was wafting from such a distance in her inner being as if it originated from the unknown, forgotten soul of her first maternal forebear.

She slid inconspicuously from the wagon and took a path which led out through the meadows past the town and into the fields.

Old Gruner had taken no notice of all that. When the first cobbles of Riedersbach were thundering under the wheels of his wagon, he recalled his passenger and turned around with the question of whether Melanie would be travelling back with him. Then he saw the empty place and no trace of her between the boards, and because he remembered the pallor and anguished expression on her face, immediately pulled the bit back in the fox's mouth so that it stopped instantly, and looked around almost in fright for Melanie Negwer. Finally he discerned her on the hill next to the town. She was striding strongly, standing tall. The scarf had slid down to her neck and the white linen carryall shimmered as if she were carrying a laced up bundle of radiant light on her back. She was too far away to call, and so he consoled himself with the thought that she had possibly been going to one of the villas behind the town on a commission, and had chosen this detour, tempted by a incomprehensible, childish whim. Although he immediately felt that this explanation did not quite fit, he paid no further attention to the soft shadow which emerged in his old soul, let the whip crack over the fox's back and rumbled slowly further into the town.

5

Lenore did not live in Klein-Pinz entirely as a stray cat; only there was hardly anyone who did not mix into their friendly words a sour little odour when they spoke with her, and she was made to feel that it would have been far better if her life had been spent travelling in the green wagon of the travelling folk to the fairs than at the Pinz waterfall house as a hidden irritation to the elders and a danger to the boys. But like all her maternal forebears, Lenore learnt to consider the doors to the residences and the natures of other people as ordinarily being for her over-grown like the trees in the forest. The whispering behind her back, she took for the rustling of the leaves, and if a boor made a coarse, smutty comment in front of her, it did not disturb her any more than if a log had fallen down next to her. In secret she held herself blameless through humble pride for the aspersions of the Klein-Pinz residents and knew, without saying a word, to put the unrelenting misfortune, which the village inhabitants in their coarseness called the prof-ligacy and the slutty nature of the Negwers, down to the effect of a higher breeding, of a finer being.

Thus Lenore thrived in the isolation of the locked-out, without the hate of the rejected, or the envy of the thrust-aside, and the only revenge she took on the Pinz residents, as an inherited trait from her maternal forebears, consisted in her never allowing her forehead to be burdened with ill-tempered creases before the others, so that no person had ever heard a complaint from her.

But now that Melanie was not forthcoming on the fourth and fifth days, her mother felt again for the first time in many years heavy in her soul that she had to live so deathly alone in the world and had nobody she could ask for advice. Really, her girl seemed to have been swallowed up by the earth or carried away in the air. Lenore did not dare to walk through the village, because she felt that Melanie's escape was already known in every house and if she let herself be seen, the windows would be too small to hold every face which looked at her full of mockery and schadenfreude. The air around her house was heated by a bitter fire, the waterfall sounded as if it were dusting clouds of ringing needles over the rocks.

Lenore only left the house at night and sat waiting at the gate because she believed firmly that Melanie would return to her from the fields in the darkness. For that reason, the poor woman sat for hours and peered through the plum trees to see if the bowed shadow of her daughter would not soon creep up out of the darkness. She did not let herself be seen during the day, kept the doors and windows closed and did not light a fire, so that the people would think the house was entirely empty. But she had erected her table in the hallway. There she spent the day in half darkness with sewing. Through the open door to the living room and the little pane over the front door, some light fell on her hands and yet she had to more feel than look with the needle.

At the end of the first week after Melanie's disappearance, Lenore's few stocks had been consumed, and in addition to all the sorrow, she now began to suffer dearth as well. But she decided to hold out past Sunday in her concealment, because she thought that with the return of the day on which Melanie had whirled out, the dazzled girl's senses would return by themselves and lead her back to her.

Sunday went past and no knuckle stirred on her door. After nightfall a large stone suddenly flew crashing against the wooden wall so that the entire house shook as if a cannon had fired, and straight afterward, little stones hailed against the roof as if a salvo of rifles were being fired at the shingles. Lastly she heard suppressed laughter running away from all sides.

After how much time she did not know, Lenore stepped cautiously through the gate under the plum trees and peered around in the weak, hazy light of the stars as well as she could, even venturing a bit into the field and taking a few exploratory steps in the furrows of the potato field, because she was of the opinion that this outbreak of the village's displeasure which had discharged over her house just then must be connected in some way with Melanie's fate and perhaps her poor child was lying, made drunk, bedraggled and defiled, behind a bush or in a ditch by the house. And every time, when she lifted branches or scanned depressions in the ground, she turned icecold in the pit of her heart and she had the feeling that someone was blowing in her face so that her it was turning black before her eyes.

On returning to the house, when she was able to distinguish the black hole of the open door in the darkness, she saw in the soft wind a bright dress wafting soundlessly through the trees and heard a whimpering as though through clenched teeth. Lenore sprang terrified over the threshold, slammed the door shut, ran into the living room and knew nothing better to do than sink down against the wall and say to herself despairingly, "There must be someone who can help me! Is there nobody in the world? Nobody, not a human soul?"

In the middle of the night, she composed herself and crept past the sleeping houses to the farmstead in which the mayor lived. But when she tried to lay her hand on the handle of the front door, she heard in herself the gruff voice of the village power, 'I'd have too much to do if I had to worry about every person who ran away and rolled around in the ditches.'

Then the woman let fall the hand which she had already raised and crept back dispirited, followed by the furious bellowing of the farm dogs she had awoken. She felt drunk with sorrow, anguish and deprivation, and with a resolution which filled her head like a swirling smoke, she wandered about for hours in the night, called for help from afar towards the shadows of the farms with a weak voice and found herself in the first grey of morning on the hill separating Groß-Mohrau from Klein-Pinz. The shingle rooves of the houses and farmsteads of the parish seat lay like grey, swollen, enormous sacks motionless in the mist of the valley. Only the church tower stood motionless and white robed, an enormous man, and looked indifferently at her with its raised onion head. Lenore felt weakly that she should walk down the hill, try to embrace the pastor's knees and ask the clergyman to help her find her girl. Now she no longer possessed the strength to do so. She turned around and hesitantly walked back along the path she had come.

In Klein-Pinz, the first smoke was already climbing out of this and that chimney. On the roof ridge of her house, however, a small, grey bird was sitting. When she passed under the trees, it came skipping to the gable projection and sang clear and terse, "Guwitt! Guwitt!", so that it sounded as if it was calling to the poor woman to "Go with! Go with!" Then it took off on its wings. At that the first tears entered Lenore's eyes. She shook her head exhaustedly, smiled bitterly and drew the door shut behind her.

6

A short sleep took the hopelessness from Lenore and, on awakening, she knew that her worries over Melanie must not turn old like dust bags in the corner of neglected houses, that she must not crawl further behind the door with her torturous waiting, but that she must set off, go out into the world and call after her vanished child.

To begin with, however, the poor woman wanted to feed herself full, that way, she thought, it would surely be easier to work herself out of the fears of her heart rand the despondency of her body.

She slipped through the door of the grocer two houses along, the widow Neugebauer, and purchased there the few things she needed to make herself full: a loaf of bread, a quarter pound of butter, sugar and coffee, and kept herself brave and poised while the old woman plied away momentously and mysteriously behind the counter with the scales and the weights. And as she had in silence half feared and half yearned for, towards the end of the pharmacist-like production, the shopkeeper grasped into the air and fetched down from there the surprise over the long absence of Melanie.

Lenore felt a piece of ice glide down her throat when the old woman began on that subject, but pulled herself together and knew to give her answers so that the departure of the girl fitted into the long embraced plan of visiting a relative, but at the same time steered them cleverly in a way which would fetch from the shopkeeper inconspicuously everything that had been gleaned in Klein-Pinz about her daughter's disappearance. Then Mrs Neugebauer packed them for her alongside the coffee and sugar, starting with Melanie's mad night of dancing in the three stalks, the suspicious, nasty, self-righteous and unkind things which had amassed in the Christians of the village, flicked in poor Lenore's ear as if by mistake that probably nobody who had two eyes in their head would believe in the tale about

Melanie's visiting, and finally said it straight to her face that everyone was convinced that the trouser-addicted girl was being kept hidden by some young man or tramp in the surrounding area and would come back when the little song had been sung to the end as was usual by the waterfall.

Lenore had to wipe the fury from her face with her hand. But hardly had the shopkeeper seen this gesture of withheld repugnance than she flew into a rage against the pride of the disreputable woman in such a way that she repeatedly heaved the bags against the counter excitedly and smashed the weights into the little basket. For various things stopped there, the old woman rattled away, for even the Holy Mother was liverish! Everyone knew that Melanie had travelled with old Gruner behind her mother's back before the first rooster's crow, still wilted and grey from dissipating the night, to Riedersbach to some such pimp of young women and now she, Lenore Negwer, came and dared to table such blatant lies — of journeys to relatives, etc. The shopkeeper flew into such a rage of wounded virtue that she overran every attempt by Lenore to respond and did not see how the insulted woman skimmed her purchases quickly into her apron and left the shop in flight. She was still blustering when Lenore was already hurrying through the garden to her house and still calling after her that she was related to the whole world.

But the worried mother paid no attention to the blustering of the old woman.

From all the trees, from all the rooves, from the wind over the fields, she suddenly heard it singing, "Guwitt! Guwitt!", and it sounded even more distinctly and urgently like "Go with!" than it had in the grey morning when she had come home half-despairing. For now she knew where to go so that she came upon her child again.

An hour later, she was striding over the threshold, equipped like her daughter, the linen carryall on her back, feeling once more for her savings in her pocket, locking the house up and placing the key under the threshold in case Melanie came home while she was absent.

The birdcall was now silenced in the world. With that she felt her breast filled to overflowing with painfully wistful maternal love, so that she ran as though carried by the wind and did not look back at Klein-Pinz anymore once she had passed the miller's hill and arrived at the hump of the plateau.

The village of Totschendorf skimmed past her like the rustling of a single garden, she sensed Heinrichau in the windless peace of summer. For Lenore was walking with bowed head and in deep thought because she was taking counsel with herself over what to do if Melanie were not to be found in Riedersbach.

She could not iron it out and just walked quicker and ever quicker as if it were favourable for her undertaking to arrive in the town in good time.

She was already standing in the square of Riedersbach before the midday bells.

The fact that her girl had been led to the county town by the whirl of her blood was construed by Lenore as proof of the noblesse of the lover Melanie had reaped in her coloured blindness. Thus she chose in the market square the opening to Wallstraße, the street which discharged its pedestrians straight from the portal of the town hall into the town square, went up to the archway of a grand house and aimed her queries at every well-dressed, important-looking man. For in relying on her great similarity in face and figure with Melanie, she thought it certain that the ardent man would have to betray himself with her unexpected look by a twitch, jerk, blanching, or such like. Then she would make straight towards him and petition him over the release of her girl.

Portly factory owners carried gold chains on fat bellies walked past the waiting woman; young, lean men with leather cases under their arms ran excitedly past her with pale faces; with loud conversation and laughter, a few distinguished gentlemen stepped out of a nearby wine bar, and when, close to the house entrance where Lenore was standing, they had merged into a narrow, listening circle for a moment because of the whispered narration of one of them, they separated with jovial whinnying, and a bold, muscular man with blond beard and red tarnished face started staggering a little and was abandoned near Lenore. There he regained command of himself, stared at her with swimming, drunken eyes for a moment, smiled meaningfully at the still pretty woman, snapped with his fingers, made a whistle with his lips and hurried after the others. Lenore watched after him, set a foot forward to set off, but shook her head smiling bitterly, drew her foot back and said with a dismissively reproving breath, "No, no ... no ... such a one? — Never!"

Not so far away, the man separated himself from the others, approached her again from the town square side, but turned into a small lane and vanished. Lenore now went to see at least in which house he entered. But on the way, all the bells in the towers suddenly started clanging the midday chimes so that the poor woman jumped in fright. From the town hall, a great horde of black-clothed men streamed and strode down the broad steps. Lenore changed her decision, moved towards them with slow, belated steps and again surveyed one after the other with attentive looks until a policeman who had been observing her for a long time approached her and asked what she was actually looking for. Lenore blanched and brought out somewhat stutteringly her intention of looking for her daughter with whom she had agreed to meet. But when the officer asked, after a critical glance over her, about what age the sought-for girl was, what she was called, and where she was from, Lenore scented a danger for her child, gave a false name, told some story, and after the policeman had left her, she took off through side streets out of the town and strolled around the country houses and villas of the suburbs, stalked back again cautiously into Riedersbach and began to ask after her daughter in the houses where she tended to sell her berries and mushrooms, scuffling in the end with pounding heart to a few houses with bad reputations and left the city on the other side in the late afternoon with a thankful feeling of happiness.

Deep in the evening, almost at night, she came to the mill between Strachat and Lindenbusch, which lay a little to the side of the main road among trees in the meadows. She was so tired that it seemed just as impossible to her to return to the village she had just wandered through as to still be able to reach Lindenbusch, and after a short hesitation, she got the better of herself and asked in the mill for accommodation for the night.

When she opened the door to the large living room of the mill, she saw, somewhat raised, in the left back corner sitting at a massive table, a greyed man and a younger, peaceful woman, obviously the miller and his wife. The former bore a long, grey beard over which a broad nose was stuck like an upside down swallow's nest. When he heard the door open, he grasped the shaded lamp hanging over the table and turned it on the entrance so that Lenore was illuminated as though by a spotlight, and wrinkled his nose with the strain of seeing.

Lenore was blinded, felt the light dip, licking over her again curiously, heard the miller's voice whisper excitedly and then heard his raw dismissal that this was not a stopping off place and you experienced little thanks from such rutting companions.

With a sigh, she turned around, saw the shimmer of the light pass by her once more and noticed on the wall bench a tall-grown, bushy haired servant who, lost in deep brooding, was whittling at the wood of the seat. When Lenore turned to the door, he lifted his head, skimmed a petulant look over her and suddenly began staring with astonished eyes, and an almost terrified look. In the same moment, she was called back by the kindhearted voice of the miller's wife and at the same time had her attention called to not falling over the steps which divided the room into a lower and an upper half.

Lenore must have given room for the conviction that she was suffering blamelessly for the wickedness of another, and when she had turned and was walking towards the table, this feeling strengthened into the narrowing certainty of being subjected to a painful inquisition. For the servant suddenly sprung stamping from his dark seat, described with his hand a dismissively furious gesture to her, let his knife snap shut loudly and set off out of the room with imprecations.

"There you have it," the miller shouted at his wife.

Lenore lowered her eyes at this indirect insult and could not stop a tear from passing through her lashes and onto her cheek. But the miller's wife, probably touched by the withheld anguish and hidden grief of the searching mother, did not let herself be misled, instead explaining to Lenore that she should not take anything from what she had heard and seen her husband and the servant say and do. It did not apply to her, but to a girl who was admittedly similar to her, like only a daughter can be like her mother. Just eight days ago, almost at the same time too, she had arrived at the mill and asked for quarter, tired, expiring, hungry, fearful and timid. If what she had said had not been all lies, then she was a poor orphan from somewhere in the mountains who was so tormented by her guardian that she finally had to pluck up the courage and go out into the world. For if she had to perish, it should at least not happen in her own village. It could happen here in God's wide world, and at that she had laughed bravely and also cried at the same time so that it called for pity. And because the harvest stood before the door and work hands were almost as hard to obtain as a third eye in your face, the suggestion was made to her by the miller to stay here and fulfil the position of a little maid. The mill lies to the side, and until people wised up to it, she could have arranged the papers from her home parish, or she could return again reconciled to her guardian.

Lenore interrupted the surging narrative by asking to be allowed to sit on the bench, for her legs were somewhat weak from all the walking. She was from Klein-Pinz and wanted to visit a relative in Mehlteuer.

At these words, the miller's wife reexamined the guest and asserted for the second time that Lenore had the same face as the maid she was talking of, only twenty years older.

"Then was she also from Klein-Pinz?" Lenore asked timidly.

"Oh no, certainly not. That is, it would be possible. Who are you then?" the miller's wife asked back.

And because Lenore had come to the dream-like certainty that the young girl the miller's wife was talking about was none other than Melanie, she hid her name from worry that the girl might have done something wrong in desperation, called herself Schröter and asked whether the stranger had perhaps been Melanie Negwer, for a relative of that name lived in the mountains.

"No, no, she had begged that we call her Anna," the miller's wife answered.

Thereupon Lenore drew her apron together with her fingers and said disappointedly and quietly, "So, so. — Yes, yes", and looked straightahead as though numbed. After a little pause, however, she got the better of herself and asked timidly what had become of the girl.

Then the miller's wife's dam burst again and Lenore learnt that it had not gone well with the alleged Anna, not well at all. Everything fitted. She had been humble, skillful, diligent and at the same time a pretty, tidy girl, and she and her husband had delighted quietly in having unexpectedly drawn such a good prize. Right up to the third day when, in mid-afternoon, she had come in pale and trembling from the field as if she had been running from a fire and behind her the servant, whom you have seen, a good, diligent young man usually, but all at once, he became almost like a devil, unrecognisable, he was waving his hands about, shouting madly, and such rude words were coming from his mouth that they should not be repeated, and all the time, he was roaring that either she must leave the house or he must.

But Anna did not say a word, fetched her carryall from her quarters, was silent, pale as a corpse, and vanished hurriedly like a shadow from the yard.

Since then the servant was as if transformed, sitting around instead of working, not sleeping at night, and when she had once said to him that perhaps such fury had arisen from spurned love, he had seemed to fall into a rage and almost attacked her.

That was the story with the girl, and it was from annoyance over the whole affair, which had lost her in the end owing to the servant, that the miller had rounded on her. But now she could stay in the same quarters in which that girl had slept, and she hoped it would turn out better than with that girl.

The miller had been silent during all that. Now he laid down the newspaper in which his eyes had been taking a stroll and rose in such a way as to make it felt that the discussion was at an end.

Lenore had completely faded away from all the seeing and hearing.

She turned down the bread which was offered to her, sought out her quarters in the lean-to and lay with large, dry eyes in a hot hum, which she could not decide if it came from the tree tops and the creek outside into her body, or if it was just the helplessness of her soul. She pressed her face fervently into the meagre pillows a few times and said pleadingly, "Melanie." But it did not help, this quiet whirling in which her entire body was floating apart did not stop.

Then a window was opened somewhere, and the miller's voice called out to the servant, whose ill-tempered voice answered from the garden.

"I am lying in the garden and sleeping!" was his mocking reply. And the window flew shut angrily.

Lenore raised herself up on the bed and asked, "Just what went on between the servant and my child?"

But whatever she thought, she found no way out and the whirling did not disappear. Through the gentle noise, seemingly as if she were lying in the night spread across the whole world and being driven apart by waves of water in all directions, she heard the servant striding restlessly throuh the grass of the garden, whistling gently for a long time and then bursting out laughing with contempt and derision. It went on without stopping. Once he came to the lean-to, sat down on something and knocked against the wood while talking incessantly to himself, dull and angry.

Then he came creeping to the door of her quarters, fumbled around at the door with softly stroking hands and whispered beggingly, "Anna ... dear ... Anna ... oh."

Only his voice sounded strange, high, crumpled by suppressed sobs, unnatural, contorted, so that Lenore thought they were the sounds of a haunted dream whose confused shadows were already surrounding her. And actually, she soon lay in the sleep of exhaustion and sorrow. The next morning, the servant saw her following her runaway daughter in the direction of Lindenbusch and Kattern.

7

Lenore Negwer and her daughter Melanie never returned again to Klein-Pinz. They went missing in the world as though in a pathless ocean.

It is only known through the servant at the Strachat mill that, the next morning, Lenore Negwer followed after her daughter in the direction of Lindenbusch and that she spent the night in the rectory at Kattern, a day's journey onward. There Melanie would also have found shelter for a short time, but no other evidence could be called up for it than Lenore's excited interview with the young chaplain of that place. Then the unhappy mother disappeared hurriedly and pale of face into the clouds of smoke of the Waldenburg coal region.

On the second day after Lenore Negwer's visit, the Strachat miller's servant, in the middle of his work, left the plough standing in the field and followed the two departed women by whom he had been struck unawares in the depth of his being. Over whether he found them, he preserved a bitter, self-deprecating silence, and after he had returned months later to the mill, he remained for a long time distant from his old self, secretive and strange, until he was lured by the radiance of another girl into his earlier assuredness.

The Negwer house by the waterfall of Klein-Pinz decayed because its owner did not return. The wooden walls turned into a heap of brown, powdery mould; the plum trees grew quickly into an impenetrable, prickly thicket, and only the elder bush on the gable side of the house facing the mountains grew up into a proper tree and spread the shade of its crown so wide that under it the untouched rubble of the house was not to be seen.

When one of the Klein-Pinz residents must walk past the maids' house, they do it in defiance or avid fright according to whether they are an old or young person, a man or woman; according to whether they believe Lenore and her daughter disappeared again into the colourful mired current of the travelling folk from whom their ancient forebear had once been washed ashore at the waterfall, or whether they leaned towards the legends which formed around the disappearance of the pair. Melanie and her mother, so they said, had returned to Klein-Pinz on a dark night after a tour of vice through all the dens and pits of the world. Ravaged in soul and body, they had drowned themselves in the whirlpools of the falls.

At low water levels, you could see at the bottom of the deeply hollowed-out pool a large, rectangular stone which was held to be the door to the subterranean residences of the monsters. The Negwer girls had been seized by them after leaping into the water and been drawn down there before they could die.

For that reason, they must live eternally.

On Advent and May nights, you sometimes see the younger, sometimes the elder Negwer maid, sitting on one of the many, large rocks which surround the mirror of water like a grey wreath of boulders. They crouch in mere shirts, singing with poignantly anguished voices old dance melodies and ringing their hands from time to time in despair until post-like arms rise up abruptly from the depths and pull them by their long, blond hair mercilessly quick into the water.

A high, shrill scream so that all the girls in the area are startled from their dreams, a short whirl at the bottom, an upwardly radiating, greenish light from the depths, and everything is again as it had been at the Pinz waterfall before the Negwer girls had settled down there.

Wendelin Heinelt

A Fairy Tale

The worker Heinelt had a wife and seven children; but because, most of the time, he had to blow on his potatoes and coffee to cool them, like at home in his father's house, his chest and cheeks had hollowed out and although illness had never afflicted him, his health was not good for all too much, and with getting by, it was if and but all of the time.

He possessed the beautiful, long name of Wendelin, and his whole life long, he could never be hung up for long, but had to be behind every pfennig like the devil behind a poor soul.

When things were not at all progressing in his home village, Wendelin thought that where the herd is large, the grazing must also be good, and moved with bag and baggage to a village which was larger than many towns. There he lived in a big house together with a hundred other people. The building looked like a monstrous, hewn, stone chest, and when people looked out its windows, you could not think anything other than that they were all prisoners.

Thus it did not actually go that well for Wendelin Heinelt here either, despite his rich name. But he did not lose his pluck, for it was the only thing that held him upright. Though he never sang, he belonged to those men who may place their mouths just so or so for it to be ready for a song.

Sometimes his eyes did not stand right in his head and all sorts of things went past on the secret waves of his soul, which he could not stop, as uncomfortable for him as it became.

He was suffering in this way one Sunday morning more than ever before. Spring had hung the first leaves on the trees. Wendelin was leaning on the fence of the little yard behind the big house. Distinguished people, women and men, and also whole hordes of children were walking along the path which ran across the field not far away and led onto the great main road which, after a few bends, disappeared into the forest. "They have it good," Wendelin thought to himself, "leaving worries and sorrows lying in the corner of their room and climbing up the mountain so that they get some air once more after being bent over the whole week long."

Where he was leaning, a maple tree was growing and as he looked up into the branches to also have a look at the great heavens, he noticed that the young leaves at the tree's top had become black and were hanging down wilted as if someone had burnt them during the night. The other trees, situated a little to the side in a trough, were free of damage. For in the night, a frost had passed through the air and had played wickedly with the maple by the fence; but the land had protected the others.

"It is for you like it is for me," Wendelin mused further, "and if I don't leave, then we, I, my wife and my seven children, will soon not have a healthy impetus in us. For is poverty no worse than frost?"

But because he could not run away so quickly, he wanted to dodge his hardship for at least a few hours and climb in the mountains like the others. So he waited for a favourable moment when his wife was in the cellar, went into the living room, furtively cut off for himself a solid piece of bread, rubbed salt on it and set off out of the room. While he was walking after the others, over the fields, along the lime tree avenue, he thought of all that he would want to buy if he ever had more money than could be held in two hands: new shirts for everyone, trousers for the boys and himself, for his wife a new skirt and if it stretched that far, a shawl with a floral edge. Above all, however, if he could have the fortune every day of having a piece of meat in the pot. The rest would work out all right. For a full stomach makes for courage. But hardly had he gone a few steps further than he tipped out the old wishes and thought of four handfuls of money and the necessities satisfied by it and the more he desired, the more unhappy he became. The people in front of and behind him were making quite a lot of noise in their festiveness, so that Wendelin could not think as he wanted to, lost the thread and got carried away. For that reason, he looked around for which path could allow him to escape the loud company the quickest. A few hundred metres into the forest, the road divided into three steep paths: to the left and right were leisurely, well levelled paths, like the way into a paradise; in the middle, there was a narrow path, abrupt and steep, right into a wilderness of stones. He continued on that path and after he had turned with the little path around a few boulders, the singing and hooting of the others sounded distant and indistinct as if it were arising from a closed pot, and Heinelt himself did not know exactly where he was. Everything had such a peculiar look about it.

"If I did not know that it is the Ochsenkopf I'm climbing up, I would probably think I'd lost my way and was in a strange land," he pondered to himself. Because he decided that he felt more at home when he thought about his wife and children and his narrow rooms, he began brooding again over his misery. But it would not work for him. Every time he looked up, it seemed to him as if the stones, which crouched so quiet and lumpish with bent backs in the moss, were springing hastily like cats over his path while he was walking so, his eyes riveted to the path. The further he went, the madder it became: the trees drew their roots out of the ground, embraced each other with their branches, like bride and groom, and were dancing up and down the mountain. The stones were leaping about soundlessly like wild rabbits. Heinelt's head was getting quite hot and he thought it was a sickness coming over him.

While he let his eyes roam around seeking help, he saw not far from himself a spacious cavern, as high as an upright man and with long stones lying like benches to the left and right. He went into it, took his colourful handkerchief out, dried his brow, then sat down and began to consume his salted bread.

He did not know he was in the place of the walking stones and, as he sat and ate, the long rock bench slowly moved with him from the spot, deeper and deeper into the cavern. To begin with, he did not notice in the slightest, because he had been captured completely by the joy of satiation. But when he had consumed the last crust, brushed the crumbs from his trousers into his hand, turned his head and carefully sent the crumbs as dessert into his stomach, he noticed with horror that he was in the middle of the mountain. He could just see the entrance to the cavern smouldering like a tallow candle. The stones, however, were moving through the mountain like hares being chased by a hound. The storms in the depths were roaring, the rocks burst cracking apart in front of him and shut thundering behind him. At every moment, he saw the wealth of the inner earth shimmering golden, silvery, in thousands of colours so that he had to shut his eyes bedazzled. He just kept holding fast onto the stone with both hands so as not to fall off, and because he had finished with life, he was not frightened so much anymore. Finally the stones went slower and ever slower. In the distance, a brightness emerged, as tiny as a mine lamp, becoming larger and larger.

At last the stone stood still and Wendelin Heinelt sat at the exit of the cavern and did not know whether this journey had really happened or whether he had just dreamed it. He stepped before the cavern and looked around. Stones lay all over the place and trees stood in between just as before.

"When you don't get anything proper in your stomach, all sorts of such weak hours come over you and you then see hell and the devil in confusion," Wendelin pondered to himself and continued along the narrow path. Suddenly a man stood before him, dressed in the style of townsmen a hundred years ago, a long coat with a lace ruff around his neck, short silk trousers, and half stockings stuck into buckled shoes. He took off his tricorn hat deferentially before poor, skinny Wendelin Heinelt, bowed deeply and then went silently along the path, always ten arm lengths ahead. The astonished Wendelin looked at him and wanted to wait until he had vanished behind a bend and then run quickly down the mountain, for it was getting a bit weird for him. The unknown man, however, turned around to Wendelin after a few steps and tapped, with the bamboo cane he held in his hand, a few times on the ground so that it seemed as if a golden bell were tolling out of the earth. The sound was so alluring that Wendelin lost all shyness and followed the strange man, because he thought it could not be all that bad and there was still time for running away. He even became a little cheerful that he had run across something strange for once in his monotonous life. His guide was striding with dignity in front of him, no different from a priest going to church, and Heinelt swallowed just in time the question whether he was also married and had children. But straight afterward, he noticed that the strange man was wearing two sorts of stockings, on the left leg a blue, on the other a red one. He thought that so funny that, without thinking much, he called, "Hey there! Good morning!"

The man immediately turned around, took the tricorn hat deferentially from his head, lowered his head and waited until Wendelin was by him.

"You surely hurried this morning in springing out of bed and into your clothes?" he asked him. The man smiled at him sadly.

"Well, I mean, you have put on blue weekday and red Sunday stockings at the same time."

The man still gave no answer.

"Well, but speak! I am just a poor devil and if something is pressing you then just feel free to say so. Perhaps I can advise you, I am, of course, Wendelin Heinelt."

No word passed over the man's lips, but his face now assumed such an anguished look as if he were carrying around the torment of seven village parishes with him under his yellow vest. With shaking head, he put his hat on again and continued on his way, his cane striking those melodious tones from the stones, which made it impossible for Wendelin to run away. The path was climbing up once more particularly steeply, the darkness of the high forest dwindled more and more, and soon they were standing at the peak, to the left and right of which, separated by saddles, other peaks closed in, larger and smaller. The tall forest had been cut away across the crest of each of the mountains as though with shears. All the southern sides, those which lay before their eyes, bore countless young saplings, each no bigger than a top hat placed on the ground. Wendelin looked at his companion standing next to him to bring to his attention how pleasant it was to look at. But he was completely rapt in the distant view of where the plain opened up between the lonely mountains: village after village separated by fertile expanses of field, rivers and lakes in between, a colourful, enchanting play, paler and ever paler until it was finally just a grey breath mixed in with the blue of the heavens. Straight after, the stranger turned to Wendelin and, after a mark of deferential respect, he walked around him and tapped with his cane on four stones which lay at the four points of the compass and looked like boundary stones, but bore stars on their upper surfaces. As soon as the ringing cane touched a stone, the stone vanished and a glorious song was released out of the deepest depths and climbed slowly upward. When the strange man had returned again to his previous position, Heinelt felt enclosed by four singing currents which poured out of the earth and straight up into the sky. From that he received a feeling as if no sorrow had ever encumbered his heart.

Full of inner thankfulness, he directed his increasingly youthful eyes at his benefactor. The latter nodded, satisfied with his success, but indicated to him with a mysterious gesture that there was still more ready to be bestowed.

He raised his cane and pointed its tip towards the far horizon. The moment it was directly opposite the grey breath of the horizon, the miracle man brought the other end to his lips and began blowing his breath into the cane. It thereby lengthened more and more, travelled across all the land and finally drilled into the haze of the most distant parts. It had turned thin, like the tail hair of a horse, and trembled in the wind.

Heinelt realised that the strange man was doing all these tricks for his enjoyment, but did not trust himself to say a word, because he was watching the little man in a great fluster. Truly, the man was not tall and Heinelt was surprised to notice this only then, for it was absurd to think that he had shrunk since he had started blowing into his cane. In any case, he did not want to lose sight of anything. The four singing currents were meanwhile flowing without stopping from the earth into the heavens. Suddenly the magician made a loud cry in an unknown language. The word became visible and fluttered like a glow-worm along the hair so quickly that it looked like a line of fire. When it hit the grey of the furthest point, there was a slight kink.

At this sign, the man brought the cane to his lips again and began to squeeze his breath into it much harder than the first time, so that his cheeks were like the angels who trumpet the last judgment. The whole world, heaven and earth, which is always like a sphere around us, seemed to be nothing but a great, colourful soap bubble on the cane of the mysterious man with the two mysteriously different stockings, who was driving his breath stronger and stronger into it. The superhuman force of his lungs split the pillars of the distant parts and shoved the walls of the horizon further and further apart so that soon the whole, entire world lay before Heinelt's eyes: all the kings and farmers, the cities complete with their mayors, not a toe or tooth was missing, not a river nor a mountain. And Wendelin did not know how to apprehend it in his astonishment. He just exclaimed constantly, "Look, the golden city! — Look, the endless green sea! — Oh, thousands of cows!" and would not have stopped at all if a groaning had not answered his joyfull cries. It became more and more desperate and anguished. Finally, with the best of will, he could do nothing but throw a glance at the magician. What he saw then was pitiful. The magician had shrunk so that he was no larger than a large loaf of bread, was trembling all over with great pain and tears were streaming over his face which was as white as the lime before the bricklayer adds sand to it. But he could not get away from the cane and had to keep blowing into it without stopping. Heinelt wanted to help him out. The four singing currents around him held him shackled and so he had to watch as, with groans, the magician blew himself more and more into the cane until he vanished completely into it. The cane pulled itself in slowly as if it were the horn of a snail, disappeared more and more into the infinity around him and soon Heinelt could no longer see any of it. The beauty of the whole world lay spread out before his brow. Only, a soft, wavering veil hung over it, which had not been there before. That is perhaps the groan of the man who spent himself on the world for my sake, Heinelt said to himself and, despite all the joy over the beautiful miracle there before and around him, an anguished emotion overwhelmed the good man. After pondering a bit, however, it occurred to him that nothing on earth goes astray, and if the magician had gone into his cane then he must surely have come out somewhere on the other side. That brought his joyful mood back and he raised his eyes again to all the inexpressible beauty of the world. But that lasted no longer than it takes to count to five on your fingers, before a transformation came over everything. The distant parts were becoming restive like a cloth that somebody was waving, rising up and down and moving ever closer.

Heinelt did not know at first what sort of cause that had. But then he saw that all the expanses were pouring into a bird with lustrous feathers which was flying straight at him and becoming smaller and smaller the closer it came. In the end, it was no larger than a blue tit, swished around his head a few times and vanishing suddenly into his ear.

Wendelin thought his head would have to burst if the whole world flew into it like that, and he crouched down so as not to fall too roughly.

But he did not fall over at all; only a dizziness clouded his consciousness for a moment. When he had stood up again, everything was as it always had been. He was standing on the Ochsenkopf, and down below beyond the forest, he saw the smoke of the chimneys and the village in which he lived.

He climbed down immediately so as to be home in time for lunch. The heels of his shoes had been moved by all the miracles to the tips of his toes; but he did not feel it. And while he thought he was hurrying home, he was distancing himself further and further from his life and stepping into the wondrous entanglements of existence.

When something great has happened to us and the soul has recovered again from its shock, then we do not know whether it was a dream or reality in which we have been blooming just then like a mysterious flower.

So it proved too for poor Wendelin Heinelt. While he was hurrying along the lime tree avenue to his village, he tried to properly account for all the events so as to know what had actually happened to him on the mountain. But he did not work it out; only as much as he sensed that he was not the same fellow as that morning, but an exceptionally competent one. His gait was easier, his head stood straight between his shoulders like a balloon which wants to climb, and his arms were no longer as stiff as carts' drawbars. The people walking past him saw none of all that and toddled along just as he had also usually done, faces turned to the ground, and searching for the previous day. Heinelt had a joy in nobody seeing his transformation, which he could not really forgive himself for. And when he came to the fence which enclosed the little yard behind the house, the landlord of the house was leaning there next to the narrow little door through which he had to go, and smoking his cigar. He was an uncouth, fat man, his face red as if coated with calf's blood and his eyes rigid as glass buttons with arrogance. His leg was propped against the doorway so that hardly anyone could get in or out. And even when Wendelin Heinelt, into whose head the whole world had flown, even when Wendelin Heinelt strode to the fence, the fat man did not draw his leg back.

'I want to see though, whether he notices anything,' the enthralled man thought, and said boldly, "Good morning. Giving yourself some pleasure too? The beautiful day really makes it worthwhile." At the same time, he looked sharply at the askew leg.

"When every ass is running around outside, I can surely lean on my fence too", the oaf answered and left his leg where it was. For better or worse, Wendelin Heinelt had to hop over the leg and the fat man laughed scornfullt behind him so that his jowls wobbled.

Sad that he had to put up with all that coarseness, Heinelt consumed his midday meal, stuffed his pipe, lay under the trees in the trough that had not encountered the frost, and thought, if the man with the different coloured stockings wanted to do him some favour, then it also could have been something else. That which he had was not enough to tinker on an old farm. Then he pondered the entire afternoon what he would choose if he knew that someone could fulfill his wishes. When the red of evening came over the sky, he was intoxicated with it, rose and crept to bed.

His wife had a cautious, pleasant nature and used her words as carefully as if they were gold coins. She probably heard her husband fetch a deep breath, but knew that he was not asleep, though he was also lying still with his face to the wall and acting like a mouse in front of the first cheese. She sat calmly and rocked their youngest to sleep while singing as quietly as if she had a flower between her lips. Then the little boy soon made a little fist and turned his little head to the side. That was the sign that the angel had taken him in its arms.

Then the wife also lay and pondered how to start to get out of him what was tormenting her good Wendelin. But nothing occurred to her; for that reason, she said on the off-chance, "If the sun keeps shining like this, the trees will soon blossom."

Wendelin, who really was still awake, sensed straightaway where that was going and thought, "She starts with Mark and she means the Lord." But because he was of the view that it was better for his wife's peace of mind if she knew nothing of the man with the different coloured stockings and the miracle cane, he gave the appearance of already being asleep and began after a while to snore quite loudly. His wife asked a few more questions quietly into the night and then settled down.

Thus Wendelin took his secret with him into his dreams and slept with it the whole night without fail. For that reason, he fell completely under its spell.

When he awoke, it was Monday and the torment was beginning again. He had overslept a little, and threw his work clothes on without looking. The coffee was already steaming on the table, a nice loaf of bread lay next to it and his wife was sitting opposite him. She looked at him furtively sometimes to work out whether he was the same as every day since their wedding.

Heinelt had been on all seven mountains that night and the good woman surely saw that in his face, but put the blame on the rush he was in. She was at hand for him in every way so that he got away as quickly as possible. On parting she pulled down gently on his cheek and said, "Unearth yourself another day."

Happy that she had not questioned him anymore, he sprang down the steps and took the path to the mine. For, around the village, there were a number of pits from out of which coal was fetched. Heinelt, who did not have enough strength and also could not do without the sun for so long, was only employed above ground. Usually he piled wood, emptied the trams and sometimes also levelled the stockpile. But he had become a navvy days before. Around the Melchior pit, as the place at which he worked was called, new buildings were being erected because a clever man had discovered an ore in the earth which was much more precious than even iron or copper, but whose name Wendelin could not retain. That was how whimsical he was.

As he thus strode to his workplace, he though about how rich and happy the owner would become if everything was successful and the steel pipes snored, and how he would already be satisfied if he could bury his poverty and everything connected with it under the ground so that it would not discover him anymore.

Thus it was clear that poor Heinelt's eyes were already not right in his head before the Lord had taken up his proper place on the sun to travel around the earth.

But on this day nothing had yet occurred. Only, when one of the directors was travelling past soundlessly in his carriage a little to the side, Wendelin propped himself up on the handle of his pickaxe, looked at the vehicle and then spat loudly into his hands as was usually necessary to fire himself up for work. When he had then let the pick go up and down for a while, he said unexpectedly, "No, it won't continue like this!" He went on in this way for three days. The fourth day was Thursday. It is an exceptionally favourable day of the week, almost as lucky as the ring finger next to the remaining fingers on the hand. His frequent conversations with himself had driven him back to work. Thus he stood somewhat to the side and toiled to dig a pitiful little birch bush out of the ground. It was small and withered and had fewer leaves than would have remained on an old bookkeeper's head. Nevertheless it did not want to be gone from the place and held so fast to the ground with its roots that the patience of the piqued Heinelt finally tore. In agitation he threw down the pick and cried, "No, it is truly no longer bearable!" As he looked up, a man came up to him and said he was absolutely right. He, Wendelin, seemed to be what you called a decent fellow. The man appeared suspicious to Heinelt because he praised him. In addition he was wearing a black felt hat with a broad rim. For that reason, he trusted him even less. He did not engage with him further, but reached for his pick again and bore down industriously on the little birch bush. But the stranger prattled like a hundred pots boiling and depicted before him all kinds of golden mountains.

Wendelin heard everything he said and when he stopped once to catch his breath, he murmured to himself, "You're also the sort to wear two different stockings." For he was convinced that all the unease and pique came from the man with the magic cane. Yes, when he looked at the round-hatted man's face from the side, he was tempted for a moment to mistake him for the magic blower himself. But with that his mistrust just grew and his grumbling became louder and louder. Finally the stranger heard how Wendelin was murmuring something all the time, and said that if it was something so bad or inappropriate that you could not say it out loud, then you should rather strangle it with your tongue and swallow it.

If someone was knocking you with rhymes, then you opened him up with your fist. Wendelin was on that score no more polite than the other, and answered that he should leave him in peace.

Completely. If he could not make him happy from head to toe, inwardly and outwardly, then he could in God's name go throw himself where the pepper grows. He did not say that quietly. The other man, however, became very polite and replied that it was quite easy to do. If he came to this little birch forest that night, fortune would be bestowed on him. But he must not forget the pickaxe.

Because Wendelin had spoken so loudly, the overseer had taken notice. He stood up from the bench, tipped the ash from his cigar and asked what was going on there.

Heinelt thought he had to keep silent over the truth, because he was frightened the overseer would swoop the fortune away before him. For that reason, he answered that a friend from his father's village was here and asking for payment of an old debt which his blessed father could not settle before his end.

"Who?" the overseer asked, very astonished, stepped quite close up to him and blew smoke into his face.

"Now, he was just standing here."

At the same time, Wendelin Heinelt turned around and wanted to point to the stranger. But the place was empty and the stubborn little birch bush had also vanished. Then a great fright ambushed the worker so that he turned quite pale and sky and earth seemed to be spinning around him. The singing currents climbed up straight out of the ground like on the mountain. It lasted no longer than it takes to brush your hair; then it was all over again.

The overseer, who knew nothing of all this, thought Wendelin was ill and was having hot flushes. For that reason, it was necessary that he go home and lie down in bed until he was better again.

He was happy with that, took his pickaxe and sought out his home. His wife closed in on him with questions about why it was that he had come home so early, but got nothing out of him. Finally he said gruffly that he was tired and wanted to sleep, and actually even lapsed into a deep sleep.

An hour before midnight, someone shook him. He turned around, but did not see anyone. Only the moon was in the sky and looking in the window with a face as if to say, "My dear Wendelin, the tale is not bad at all." For that reason, Heinelt rose very quietly, grasped the pickaxe, crept out of the house and was soon in the little birch forest.

It was a night as light as day. The birches were standing quite still, so still that you could hear the moonlight flowing over the leaves like a silvery stream of air. Wendelin walked between the white trunks, felt down the velvety inner bark and breathed the scent of the young leaves; but he saw and heard nothing of the stranger.

Then the bells in the village below tolled the twelfth hour. Each strike hummed for a while in the tower until it had found its way out. But in travelling out, it became a white bird with broad wings, as large as a swan. Each one struck the air with its white wings so that it tolled through the high heavens right up to the stars and made them tremble. Then the draught flowed into the little forest, one ringing bird after the other, as if they were real wandering swans. They described a few circles over the tree tops of the birches, then shot straight down so that it looked as if a shimmering rope was falling from the blue sky and vanishing in the branches not far from him.

Instantly a great stillness reigned again, yes, it seemed to him as if breathless expectation lay in the air so that, to start with, he did not dare to lift a finger. Yet as the anxiety had fallen away from him, he just tiptoed from where he was to the place where the white birds had disappeared. The branches of the birches rose and fell shaking and the tiny leaves trembled like a silvery veil above.

Shaking his head, Heinelt said, "But the birds could not have gone into the ground." But because too many wondrous things had happened to him already during the day, he bent down to the ground and looked at the young grass which covered the ground. But it was fast asleep. Each blade was bending a little and a tiny little drop hung on its tip as if it were crying in its dream. Then a little weakness of heart came over good Wendelin, because he thought the grass was sad for him, that he, son of a righteous mother, was wandering on such paths. In order to finally break free of this enchantment, he passed his fingers through the blades and wet his eyes with the moisture. But hardly had the midnight dew wet his eyes than he felt like a cobweb was falling from his eyes and his ears were unlocked. From the grass, he heard a voice which sounded like the chirping of summer crickets on distant field margins. A blue, pale fire came out of the earth and illuminated the green grass from below so that it looked as if it were growing on a restive wide flame. When he looked closer, he noticed that the blades were moving as if a lazy bumble-bee were creeping through the green.

"Now luck is coming", Wendelin Heinelt thought, seized the handle of his pickaxe tighter, and squeezed his breath into his chest.

It was next to the tuft where he riveted his eyes, though, a bare place on which only moss grew, and a few dry winter leaves lay there. The stirring of the stalks came closer and closer to the more open space, and the faded voice let itself be heard anew. But now it sounded short and surly like a wagoner's call driving a tardy animal.

Another little voice answered, gently singing like the wings of a playing midge and exulting in the air. Before he could wink once, a little, little wee man, naked and blood-red, stepped out of the tuft of grass. His thin legs ended in little mice feet and behind he had a hairless little tail, thin as a root hair. A long, yellowy-white beard hung from his ancient, wrinkled face; on his head, moss grew instead of hair and his eyes glowed faintly from eternal sorrow.

He was pulling a grasshopper on a dry blade behind him. It was drowsy, propped itself on a little leg and obdurately lowered its antennae.

Now it was fortunately out of the blades. When Wendelin saw on its back a being, he was astonished that there could ever be something so small. It was quite like the little man, but was no longer than a flour beetle. Then Heinelt knew that he had come among the root men who tend the little seeds of the earth and guard the door to all subterranean treasures, and he strained to hold his breath even longer, because he hoped to learn something from their conversation which could be useful to him.

The grasshopper was still resisting and did not want to go on at all. For that reason, the old root man began singing again with his chirping voice,

> Trembly, hairy, weakling,
> Get on quicker, lazy thing;
> Sun yourself by day and lie and squint:

Now I want to ride our prince.

But Heinelt could not with the best of will hold his breath any longer and let it burst out. The little root men were scared to death. The old man emitted a squawking shout, tore the little one from the steed and vanished through a crack in the earth. He heard them clattering down screaming, grasped his pick, wet the tips with the night dew and hewed into the ground where they had both vanished so that only sparks were thrown up. The clods which he hacked out were falling back again and again and closing up the entrance to the depths; but he did not slacken. Sweat appeared on his brow, his arms trembled, but the hole became larger and larger. The light from below increased and finally he came to a broad stone which looked like a trapdoor.

He paused for a while and listened to the tangle of fearful little voices whirring about underneath in great confusion. But the longer he rested, the more the noise of the little root men calmed down and the thrown out earth began slowly to trickle down the walls of the hole again. Thus Wendelin realised that if it just continued for a short time, the opening would soon be closed up again.

Every sympathy with the distress and fear of the little earth spirits immediately disappeared and, with the mood of a blind, ravenous appetite, he hewed with the head of the pick against the trapdoor to smash it to pieces if it would not open for him.

After the seventh blow, a little grey man stood in the middle of the stone, holding his little white hands up above himself protectively, and looking at him so that the poor fortune seeker was seized by a feeling mixing fright and awe. Whether he wanted to or not, he had to immediately place the pick next to his leg and observe the little man who, without looking at him further, had taken a seat and inclining his face to his white hands which lay closed next to each other.

"What do you want from me?" the little man asked after a long silence, raising his head and looking deeply at Wendelin Heinelt.

"Take your look off me, I can't bear it," he answered; for the fright was beginning to overwhelm him.

The grey man lowered his face to his hands and asked again, "What do you want from me?"

"The fortune", Wendelin finally brought forth haltingly.

"Your fortune or that of another?"

"No, my fortune."

"That I cannot give you, that you must seek yourself. But the eyes that look for it and find it, that you can have if you don't want anything else. Grasp it without hesitation. Don't let it out of your hand as soon as you have seized it. — I also want to tell you of a sign by which you can recognise it: as soon as you have found your fortune, the eyes which looked for it will be blinded so that you no longer recognise it."

He rose, threw a little, golden snake from his hand and was no more to be seen. Wendelin bent down quickly and seized the golden creature. It was burning so that its body blazed like a fire. But when he had enclosed it inescapably within his hand, it became a round, cold, slippery ball, no different from the eyeball of a dead man. But the stupor which God graciously wrapped around his senses was taken from them in the same moment and he saw and heard everything as it was.

That bewildered poor Heinelt in deepest amazement. For, although it was night and remained so, everything lay in a pale, smouldering light streaming up from the earth into the dark sky like the smoke of a hidden fire. In the fields, this breath was light and peaceful. Trees and bushes slept in dark, inner night and thin threads of light poured down on them from the stars. Over the village on which Wendelin now riveted his eyes, this mysterious brightness smouldered stronger, more restive, sicker. For a while, he hesitated to stride down into this shimmer which lay like a quivering shroud over all the rooves.

"But, whoever has said A must also say B", Wendelin said to himself, pulled himself together and strode lustily downhill. When he arrived between the houses, he noticed that the light which lay over everything was coming through the pores of the brick walls like painfully glowing drops of sweat and at the same time, he heard coming through the house walls the confused voices of the dreams which were visited on the sleepers in their beds. If he had just listened to it for a quarter of an hour, he would have lost his mind or would have had to have thrown the eye of fortune away. Only he wanted neither the one nor the other, but ran as quickly as his legs could carry him across the street, down the little lane, across the yard and up the stairs to his room. When he finally lay undressed in his bed, he wondered how he had managed to come in without waking any of his family. But hardly had the fluster from running died down in him and he had set himself properly to go to sleep, than the eye of fortune began to take effect in his room. Heinelt immediately sat half up in his bed. Although the room was dark, his wife and children lay visible in their beds. The desires of their hearts were smouldering from within and illuminating them; at the same time, the voices of their dreams were sounding from their chests. The little room was so suffused with sobbing, laughing, singing and loud cries that he was frightened his wife might be woken by the racket and ask what it was. Then he would have to tell her everything, show her the eye of fortune, and all his fear would then have been in vain and he would have to remain poor Wendelin until his last breath. This thought brought the sweat onto his forehead. For he noticed well that it was not working out. Meanwhile the entire big house was shaking louder and louder from the din of the dreams. For in addition to the landlord, many other oafish people lived there and their souls were making a racket in their sleep like empty dogcarts on rough cobblestones. In his fear, Heinelt grasped his eldest son's kite string, which lay in a ball on the window sill, and ran down the steps into the yard. There an old well lay scantily covered with boards in the corner behind a stack of mine timbers. Wendelin went to it, pulled a board away and bound the eye of fortune up with the string so that it could not slip away.

"I want to leave it in the well. If it hangs in the depths from which it came, the houses will lie dark and the dreams of men will remain calmly in their bodies. But I will stretch out so that I can learn in my sleep what I should do."

Thus he let his eye of fortune down on his son's kite string into the old well. But as the eye went under the ground, deeper and ever deeper, it increased in weight and was finally so heavy that the string would have to break any moment. Wendelin toiled in vain to draw it up again, it hung as heavy as a church bell. His arm trembled, the string snapped. So as not to lose his life's fortune, the desperate Wendelin jumped down into the well himself.

He lost consciousness and when he came to below, it was a dusky grey like it is with us before the sun climbs over the mountain, and he could see as far below himself as above. Thus he found himself between two abysses. In front of himself, he saw a bright, wide band running out, it was a path which he wanted to walk. The eye of fortune lay next to his left foot and shimmered reddish up at him. He bent down to pick it up. Then it seemed to him as if another white arm reached out for it from the thick haze which lay around everything. Wendelin kicked at it with his foot and the greedily crooked hand melted away like a shadow while a restrained cry of pain rang out, dying out after a short tremor in such harrowing anguish that Heinelt hastily gather up his eye of fortune, threw the kite string away and ran off down the path without looking.

He ran and ran. All at once, it seemed to him as if thousands of other men were around him, striving for the same goal as him. Wherever he turned his eyes, right or left, in front of or behind himself, the outlines of other men shimmered indistinctly towards him, as if wherever he stood, he was opposite a deep pool and seeing his image in it.

Although Wendelin Heinelt had experienced so many wondrous things, a hidden horror overcame him anyway. He drew his head in and ran as fast as he could. In the distance, it was starting to smoulder brightly, becoming brighter and brighter, as if dimmed lamplight were falling through a grating. When he came closer, he noticed that it was a giant tree stretching its leaves far outwards and upwards. The leaves were formed like the breathing mouths of men and the branches lay so thickly on each other and were so ironhard that it was impossible for poor Wendelin to slip through. For that reason, he took the eye of fortune in his left hand. Hardly had he closed his fingers around it than it began to stir and rushed at the tree with such violence that Heinelt could not resist.

He covered the few steps to the trunk stumbling, pressed his balled right fist against the bark and cried heartily, "I am Wendelin Heinelt. Whoever is keeping the tree's door shut, I ask, open it for me!"

Then a roaring went through the leaves, the tree opened up and Wendelin was torn through it by his eye of fortune. That happened very fast and the noise was also in his body. When the tree shut again with a loud roar, Heinelt did not know if the flight had taken a year or a second. His body was still shaking in the air current which had carried him, so that everything was revolving about him. At the same time, a droning like the voices of countless men was around him. He raised his head in astonishment and found himself in a round hall which was as large as a world. Its walls were formed by trees like that through which his eye of fortune had driven him. Thousands upon thousands of trunks were constantly opening up and from all sides, people were streaming in: men and women of every age and class with the exception of children. At a quick run, arms thrown up, eyes wide open in fervent longing, they plunged into the middle of the enormous hall of the underworld.

Some were scurrying like the wild animals of the fields; others had sweat on their brows and were going slowly from their places. Those strong ones for whom their lingering was blocking the way ran over them and pushed them down with hands and feet. As soon as one of the downtrodden touched the ground with their chest, he dissolved into smoke which was sucked up greedily by the earth. This merciless struggle rampaged without stopping. Only a few of the thousands upon thousands who had been drawn through the lively trees reached the middle of the hall. There the little heap of chosen ones stood still and they raised their foreheads and hands up. For the ceiling vaults of the hall, which built themselves up grey and airy like climbing smoke, had in their heights a round opening through which supernatural light flowed down onto the waiting ones.

Heinelt, who saw all this, was so seized by the wonders of the lower world, above all by the fate of the downtrodden, that he completely forgot he was looking for his fortune and directed his eyes full of sympathetic curiosity at the few people in the middle. He had worked out that fortune would probably come from the opening up above.

But before he himself risked his life to reach there, he wanted first to wait and see what else would take place. Directly opposite him, in the outermost row of waiting people, a beautiful youth was standing, lean and blond. He was still so worn out from the murderish run that he could barely stay on his legs, and his raised arms constantly threatened to fall down. Now the exhaustion was bowing his body to the earth so that his locks were almost touching the ground. His face was quite extinguished and it seemed to be quite indifferent to him whether the earth sucked him up or not. Then a cry of jubilation went through the elect. From the shimmering heights, a shining flame slowly came down and hovered for a moment over the heads of the waiting people whose arms were raised twice as ardently. The bowed youth tore himself up with

his last strength and as he stretched his arms upward, the flame passed down and vanished into
his open mouth.

He immediately raised a heavenly song that
filled the dark hall of expectation with golden
floods of light. To the right, the grey horizon tore
open and you could see the entire world of men
lit by the sun towering up into the heavens.

The blessed youth strode there with floating
steps, his arms spread out wide. The closer he
came to the cities of life, the more beautiful and
sublime they became from his tireless song.
Their rooves dripped with gold, the forests
stirred in clamouring melody, and the people on
the paths walked about like the saved. Then he
had vanished.

The grey wall closed again and the hall of expectation lay as oppressively as before. But
Wendelin Heinelt did not know what sort of fortune had befallen the youth and looked around
to see whether there was a man who could tell
him. He looked up and down the wall of trees. Finally he caught sight of a man to his left who, as
poorly dressed as him, was leaning next to the
tree from which he had come and obviously did
not trust himself either to go across to the
middle. He stood humbly, with lowered face and
yet there was such a wondrous thing about the
man, an incomprehensible majesty, that

Wendelin did not dare to talk to him, but looked at him and could not take his eyes from him.

"The youth received the fortune of song", the stranger said unbidden to Heinelt, nodded to him cordially and then directed his attention back to the middle. Wendel looked there too and resolved to himself that if the good man ran to the light then he would try as well. He wanted to run on the tips of his toes and if he stumbled, he would do a somersault in the air so that he did not fall and be sucked up by the earth as smoke like so many others.

But he did not have need to, for suddenly such a powerful blow happened to the vaults of the world-wide hall that it trembled like the mirror of a pond. Wendelin turned his head to the good man to ascertain whether it meant something good or bad. But before he could notice what sort of face he was making, another blow followed and then another and each was more violent than the previous one. It seemed like the most terrible storm Wendelin had ever heard was striking with its fist on the roof of the hall of subterranean expectation. But with each blow, the bluster of a storm as encountered in the mountains did not flow. No, the roaring which came down in ever new blows from up above formed itself more and more distinctly into the storm of a tremendously beautiful music. The vaults became lighter and lighter and finally radiated in the glow of a blessed mid-spring day.

Heinelt was possessed like in church. He knelt down and clasped his hands. When he finally dared to raise his eyes, he noticed with fright that the great flashing vaults of the hall were joined together by glaring, living eyes and each of the leaves of the wall which enclosed the enormous space was a mouth moving in song.

"They are the eyes and mouths of the downtrodden who were sucked up by the earth", poor Heinelt thought and crawled a little further away on his knees so that he did not disturb the singing leaves. All at once, the song fell silent, the eyes of the vaults glowed even more and from the opening above the middle, a stream of fire came down with such fervour on the elect that Wendelin sprang horrified onto his feet because he thought the poor people would be burned up by it. But when the sheaf of fire was hovering thickly over their heads, it vanished into their bodies. After that they all moved with floating steps like the blessed youth to that side where the wall of the hall burst apart and showed the city of life. There they passed away, like clouds melting away in a hot summer sky. They died right into heaven and immortality, for from each something remained behind which exalted the beauty of life. From this soul flowed a house, shimmering white and regal behind dark greenery; from that soul, the forests drank a deep green, the seas a deep blue; others were exhaled into the sky above, and the arc of heaven stretched further, the face of earth became more distinct and the songs in the air more sacred by their happy demise.

In the end, everything was extinguished like a dream in sleep. The wall had leaves, the vaults grew grey like climbing smoke and the entire enormous hall lay in dismal, oppressive dusk. But from the circular opening up above the middle flowed a white, peaceful light.

Wendelin, who had observed everything in breathless suspense, pulled himself together and turned around; for his heart was really aching.

"If I could only pass through the wall again, I would surely find my way back to the well, climb up my son's kite string to the yard and ask no more for my fortune", Wendelin pondered. "For those who don't reach their fortune vanish like smoke into the ground and those whose yearning is fulfilled, pass away like a breath in the wind. What sort of difference between fortune and mis-fortune is that?"

He grasped in his trouser pocket and could not find the kite string anymore, for he had thrown it away out in the haze of people before the tree. Now his anguish was even greater. He would have liked most of all to throw himself to the ground in order to die. Only, in good time, he thought of his children who would go hungry if he passed away down here. His dear wife would certainly cry until she went blind. For that reason, he wanted to attempt what thousands upon thousands had attempted before him. He felt the eye of fortune still in his hand, turned around and looked at the opening up above in the middle of the vaults. Then he clenched his teeth together, balled his fists and lifted his body onto the tips of his toes to run. Then in the opening above, a pale, ancient face appeared that was so beautiful that Wendelin thought it must be God himself. The old man smiled at him in great affection and a tear of joy fell from his eye. It sank from his cheek and floated for a while luminously in the air. Then it flew slowly to him. Just before Heinelt's forehead, it shot to the side and hit the good man who had so readily given information in the middle of his chest. He immediately emitted a high-pitched scream, grasped desperately with his hands in the air and began to fall to his knees. But before he could touch the ground, Wendelin had caught him in his arms. He laid the smitten man, whose body was as slack as a dead man's, carefully and gently across his left shoulder and walked as if it thus pertained to him and no other to go across the hall to that side where the city of life lay. When he came to the wall, it burst apart by itself and the whole world with its thousands of blue mountains, hundreds of sparkling cities, endless oceans and inexpressible songs under the sky above lay before him, just as magnificently as the magician on the Ochsenkopf had blown them from his cane. A broad road led into the middle of it and the stones on its edges were of pure gold.

Before Heinelt took the first step on it, he looked back once more into the hall. At this moment, the millions of eyes in its vaults smouldered and the leaves opened and sang a song of jubilation which rang powerfully like the roaring wind of a storm.

Heinelt rejoiced over the beautiful song which was being sung to him and would have liked to hear it to its end. But he thought of the wounded man that he was carrying and stepped forward lustily in bare feet so that he could put him up in the first house he came to. But hardly had he taken a thousand steps than the ill man tapped him affectionately on the back. Wendel stood still. The wounded man climbed down from his shoulder and stood quite soundly before him.

Then Heinelt saw that it was really the magician from the Ochsenkopf who had blown the whole world for him from his cane, and he remembered his eye of fortune which had vanished. His hands were empty and even all around, there was nothing to see. For that reason, he looked disconcertedly at the magician.

But the latter said, "You did not take care of your fortune, in order to stand by me, and did I not tell you this, that your fortune shall be invisible from the moment when you possess it?"

Wendelin wanted to remark humbly just then that not he, but the little grey man on the stone had said that, but found no time for that, for the magician had pulled a golden stone from the edge of the road, stepped up to him, and gave it to poor Heinelt, and then brushed his right hand over both eyes of the receiver. Wendelin stammered words of thanks and because he had no hands free, instead of squeezing the magician's hand, he squeezed the golden stone to his chest. In this moment, he was torn away. It went so fast that he had to shut his eyes. When he opened them again, he lay at home in his bed. It was a bright, joyful morning. The whole world was looking in the open window. The leaves of the trees were singing like the mouths of men and the sky was as blue as if it were made up of countless, deeply inspired eyes. But from all that, a countenance of sublime goodness dawned in a mysterious way.

His wife bent over him and asked in distress where he had been.

Wendelin Heinelt laughed with all his heart, pushed the covers back and showed her the golden stone which lay next to him. It had turned into a beautiful, round loaf of bread, brown, cracked and fragrant like those they fetched every day from the baker.

The risen man summoned all his children and after all had eaten from the bread, they felt as full of delight as if they were in paradise.

So it remained right up to the present day, the bread had no end and whoever ate from it received a golden heart full of happiness and affection and their eyes remained large and gentle.

Heinelt had yet more sons and daughters. All had the same look, the same joyful, quiet mouth.

Even you have now and then seen one of his family. If you ask someone for a drink of water and he offers you the jug; for a bite to eat and he offers you the loaf; for a corner for your head and he offers you his house, then you know it is a child of that Wendelin Heinelt who went in anguish searching for his fortune and when he had found it, did not take care of it, just so he could help his poorer brother.

One day, however, we will all become Heinelt people. Then heaven will be on earth and nobody will be frightened by death anymore.

The Fire

In the loft of the largest tavern of a small country town, the young maidservant was, with the help of a candle she had stuck to the top of her clothes basket, singing her hair in order to play a fitting role in the festive wedding party down below in the saloon. But her mop of hair was unruly and her vanity insatiable, and so it happened that she could not get the business straightened out. And when she was finally called for urgently, she threw the hot shears angrily to the ground, left the light burning and ran down grumbling into the saloon again.

As the merriment of the boisterous party was climbing, the candle in the maidservant's room burnt down further and further until the flame seized the braids of the basket and, just as the dance was starting in the hall below with a fanfare for the bride and groom, the fire penetrated down the building's loft hatch and a few moments later, the roof timbers were in full blaze. Screaming, the party plunged out onto the street, the fire horn tooted fearfully through the lanes of the town, and after barely half an hour, the first firemen were racing on the fire-engine to the place of the misfortune. The entire street stood wedged full of the curious, mostly workers from the factory nearby. Their eyes played in the glow of the flames, and were full of satisfied curiosity.

Their hands in their pockets, idle and full of contentment, they stood there, just as if there were fireworks in progress before them. Meanwhile the fury of the devastating flames was growing under a light breeze. The fire-mice were running along the entire roof ridge and springing down the stairs onto the second floor and threatening to ride onto the rooves of the neighbouring buildings. In this adversity, the beset firemen turned to the workers who still filled the lane, idle and comfortable and often letting their mouths hang open with pleasure, and asked with moving, earnest words for them to stand by the unfortunate townsman and the threatened town and finally intervene actively with them. But that went down beautifully with the good men. At first the workers drew back grumbling, then they raised a mocking laughter across the board, and finally one of them shouted loudly, "Sh...! Let the joint burn down. Bravo, all the rich should go that way!" And without stirring a hand, the entire pack skived off into the next lane.

This story is not invented. It happened three weeks ago in a Silesian town.

But the criminal lunacy does not rule just over the short-sleeved men of this town, it is the ill-fated spirit which has captured the entire German workforce. The prosperity of the entire folk is being transformed quickly as though by a devastating fire into smoke and ashes, and soon everything will lie in rubble. Only, instead of helping to stem the calamity with strong fists, the workforce is standing idly by, yes, even with schadenfreude and letting everything decay because they do not know that, along with the possessions of the rich, their existence will also be destroyed until nothing more will remain for them than to nourish themselves on robbery and murder.

For anyone who wants to live must work, either in the honourable enjoyment of faithfully fulfilled duty or in the drudgery of crime. There is no other choice.

The Gotschdorf Woman

A Christmas Tale

Hermann Stehr

In the weeks before the last Christmas of the Great War, the villager Antonie Nagel, a poor woman from the village of Gotschdorf in the district of Hirschberg, was preparing breakfast for her four children. She plied her life as strenuously as the many mothers whose men were in the war and who could only choke with gaunt hardship through the costly times. When the children had drunk the thin coffee and devoured the meagre bread, the poor woman surely saw that none of them were properly full. But if she had yielded to her heart and fed the children until their eyes glowed, they would have all been confined indoors on this and the following day with an empty bread bin. That is why she left the room, because she could not bear the yearning faces of her children. She opened then the bin, saw the half loaf which she still had, made a short, but hard battle with her maternal love and finally said, "No, I must not yield to my sympathy! If my Johannes is lying outside in the Russian trenches in the cold, in danger and always near death, then we at home will surely be able to deny ourselves something." Only hardly had she spoken the words to herself than an indescribable aching rose in her heart so that she paid no attention to her brain, held the half loaf in her hand, went back into the room, grasped the knife and cut the bread up small right to the last crust. "There, children, eat. If the hardship comes from God, he will surely send us help too." At the same time, she smiled to them so lovingly that the children overcame their timidity and set about the mountain of slices until nothing more was on the table but the small crust. But nobody touched it because they knew that she would have liked to have had it for herself, although she voiced not a word of desire for it. Instead the poor mother stood at the table and delighted over how her four were eating like Turks. For they were four boys, each a hand taller than the next, fresh and brown, and the oldest almost reached to her shoulder. As they now sorted out their bags to go to school, the woman suddenly thought it silly to keep the crust of bread for herself, and she cut it into four pieces, compelled each to take his piece and pushed them out the door. When the four hurried down the small garden to the street, she called to them that if she were not yet there when they came home, they should not have any fear. For she wanted to go down to Warmbrunn to see whether anything was to be earnt there.

Then the woman watched after them for a long time until they had vanished between the trees and houses. On going back inside, it became dark with sorrow before her eyes, and whether she wanted to or not, she had to think,

'How soon, one after the other will go out of the house and never come back again. For wherever you turn in this frightful life, there stands death.' She was at once fed up with this thought, sat down at the table, pushed the plates across the top, placed her head on her arms and began crying soundlessly, without sobs, from the depths of her soul. And whenever she tried to pull herself together, a new dark wave rose up in her so that her eyes overflowed again.

Then it suddenly seemed to the poor woman as if someone were tapping with the nail of their finger on the windowpane and saying with an exhausted voice, "Come and help me!" Jerking up and thinking it was a sign from her man was all one. She stepped to the window, looked out into the frost covered garden and finally called out, because everything remained empty and still, "Who is out there then?" But her apprehension became still stronger from her own fearful voice, and it beset her that perhaps the worst had happened to her husband at this moment, and his soul was taking leave of her and his home town in this mysterious way. Reeling, she went out, walking through the village as if with woolsacks on her feet. She could not take three or four steps without saying to herself, "Johannes has not written for four weeks, and today he tapped me."

Thus poor Nagel went past the inn at the bottom end of the village and entered the main road which was planted with tall maples to the left and right. A quite strong wind had risen, and the empty crowns roared as if an endless series of rumbling wagons were passing ahead of her through the air. The Sudeten Mountains stood like an abrupt wall, vertiginously steep up into the air, and the mountain inns on the ridge were like lonely men straying about helplessly and seeking an opportunity to spring into the heavens. On the Stonsdorf heights, she spotted a tree, solitary and covetous on the peak of a bare knoll as if it had already drawn its roots from the earth and was waiting impatiently to fly away in the wind with the umbrella of its crown, never to be seen again, as if everything desired to abandon this insecure earth and emigrate to another world. Wherever poor Nagel directed her eyes, she saw everywhere not the world as it is, but only the sorrow, the unease, and the fearful images of her heart. For that reason, she lowered her eyes again and thought, 'Whoever looks in front of their feet walks the most securely', and the sorrow with which the war was making music through hundreds of thousands of poor German women, Nagel from Gotschdorf just had to overcome that too. But hardly had she gone past two maples at a steady gait than she began again, despite the rumbling treetops above her, to listen to her own steps; not long, she counted again to four, her eyes ran full of water, and the thought that her husband had been stilled forever that morning in Russia seized her hotly like the embers of a stove. She had to sit down on a milestone, and because her heart was labouring too much in her, she doubled up about her knees to prevent it bursting in her. 'I cannot and must not die', she thought. 'For the time being, it is nothing but fear. But if it extinguishes me, then my four boys will be alone in the world, and hardship will be their mother and hunger their father.'

But when she stood up again after a while, the sky was burning a deep red over the mountains on the other side of the Hirschberg's peak, and clouds were chasing over it like black riders. Everywhere it pecked at the sky like it had before on the panes of her window, and it again seemed to the poor woman as if it were calling for help behind every hill, every mountain, even every mound of earth.

"Yes, if only I could", Nagel said, "I want to help and even if it draws the blood from under my nails. Just my husband, my Johannes, must not die for me."

As Nagel thus said that to herself and let her eyes wander about searchingly, it seemed to her as if something was coming from behind the bulge of the earth towards her. Only it was going and going and was yet not be seen. Then the Gotschdorf woman sprang over the ditch and strode into the field to a small birch tree standing all alone on a mound and moving its reddish crown of rods as if it were waving to the poor woman to come and look from there out into the distance. Hardly had Nagel stepped next to the little tree than she caught sight of a man coming slowly and laboriously up the next wave of hills, bare-headed, his head lowered, and propped on a stick which had been quickly broken from a bush. His coat fluttered in the wind, and the wanderer grasped in vain with his free hand again and again for its ends. Hardly had he caught it and drawn it across his chest than the clothing was pulled from his powerless hands by a new wind gust and again whipped about the man who was as gaunt as if he had issued from an ossuary. The red of the sky and the chasing of the black clouds were also around him in an inexplicable way. Now the man had caught sight of the woman. A delighted smile slid across his emaciated, pale face, and she noticed how he was straining to reach her. But he only progressed a few steps. Then his knees bent more and more, he began to sway and collapsed a few field widths from her by two boulders which towered up out of the ground between two rowan trees in a broad field margin.

When something unexpected happens to us or an incident takes shape which we alone feel and which passes incomprehensibly through our secret heart, then we surely pause in the certainty of whether what confronts us is reality or just a spectre of our eyes. In this way, Nagel was not certain either whether she had just seen in truth an exhausted man or a ghost in broad daylight which collapsed into nothing when she passed her cool hand over her eyes. Nonetheless, she did not hesitate for a moment, but ran without thinking straight across the winter sowing to the two trees. The closer she came, the more distinctly she heard the groaning of the poor man and saw as she hastened to the field margin that, lying on the ground, he was grasping at the boulders with his hands to straighten up.

"Remain lying easy! Don't strain yourself!" the Gotschdorf woman called to him, "I am coming and will help you." Perhaps it is an escaped prisoner from Lauban, she thought. But what harm is that? If I only do what I can, God will ensure good comes to my Johannes. Then she had arrived by the man who lay with his face to the ground and only breathed weakly and whistling. As it lay in her steadfast way, she did not bother at first with all sorts of delicate words, but bent down to straighten up the pitiable man and lean him against the boulder.

"For God's sake, woman, don't move me!" the man cried softly, having sensed her movement, and tried to move away from her grasping hands.

"But you cannot lie with your face on the cold ground!" Nagel said reproachfully, paid no mind to the resistance of the exhausted man, instead bending down to succour him against his will. Only, even before she could touch him, the poor man propped himself against the earth, came up arduously and leant with his back to one of the boulders.

"Who are you then and where do you come from?" Nagel asked shaking when she saw his face which was more bones than skin.

Breathing out, he answered with something which sounded like "everywhere", but had to fall silent again straightaway, for his emaciated body was shaken by a convulsion so that she heard his teeth chattering, and then a stream of black blood flowed from his mouth, pouring in jerks and not stopping at all, so that Nagel thought in horror, "Jesus Maria, he is dying!"

But the blood finally stopped flowing, and the man leant exhausted against the stone to rest a little from the attack.

A slumber seemed to scurry over his eyes which lay so deep in their sockets that they could not be seen.

The Gotschdorf woman had to turn away in emotion from this image of sorrow which looked almost like horror. When she dared to look again, a bitter smile lay over the bone yellow face of the fatally ill man, and his mouth moved, but Nagel could not hear anything.

For that reason, she asked, "What are you wanting to say? I will do all that you ask of me. So just speak."

With that he bent down.

"Woman", the poor man said almost inaudibly, "be happy that you are human. You have it good. You can at least die ... But go away so that my breath does not touch you."

Shocked, the woman leapt up, took a step back and asked, "Why do you say 'human' to me? What are you then, man?"

But the stranger had already let his head fall powerlessly again, and she heard his breath going like a weak flickering in his chest.

"Man", the Gotschdorf woman said, "if you don't want to be human, what else do you want to be?"

Nagel spoke loudly now so that it echoed across the fields, for she was frightened for one, and, for another, she thought the invalid was talking madly and would perhaps come to his senses again with her strong voice. And the stranger actually answered clearly and distinctly, "Good, I will tell you. But beforehand you must promise me that you will do for me what I ask of you." And when Nagel had assented, he said, "Now go first and sit down on the other boulder."

After that had also happened, he spoke, always with lowered head, "I know well that you are a good, strong German woman. But what I have to say could play tricks on you. For that reason, hold firmly with your hands to the rowan tree."

After that he waited a short while, lifted his head a little and looked obliquely over to Nagel, who sat with pale face on the boulder with both arms slung around the tree trunk and looked at him anxiously full of expectation.

"You know, woman, I cannot continue anymore", he then said.

"From hunger, right?" the woman asked.

"No, because I have no hunger anymore, because I am full up to the neck, to bursting. You saw it before. Everything I enjoy, I must again give of myself", the stranger spoke with lamenting voice.

"But no", Nagel interrupted him, "you have burst blood. You are no animal."

"That no", the stranger replied, "but I am death."

The Gotschdorf woman was so frightened by these words that she was torn into a deep powerlessness. The stone on which she sat whirled with her into the darkness, up high, church tower high. When she came to her senses again, it seemed to her that she had had a terrible dream about death. She opened her eyes, saw the man, who actually looked to a hair like an emaciated, exhaustedly trembling vagrant, still sitting there and she asked disbelieving, "So you are death?"

But she ignored the silent affirmation of the terrible man, quickly considered all the strange things which had happened to her from early that morning, found that she could not actually have met anyone else today but death himself, was again beset by vertigo from the horror, sprang up and ran away.

Death, sitting behind the boulder, did not stir, for he well knew that Nagel would not run far.

She had also not yet entirely run all the way down the field margin when it occurred to her that death had asked her for something, and if he had already pushed her Johannes into the grave then he would not have done that. If she thus went and asked, she might be able to rescue her husband.

That is why she returned, stood from a distance and waited timidly.

"I felt it in my heart that you would return, woman", he said and smiled peacefully.

"Has it gone so far with me, death, that you already beat in my heart?" she asked trembling.

"Don't cry, I am in every heartbeat of every human from birth onwards. But you are not yet finished, not you and not your husband. So have no fear. I possess power only over those whose lives are finished. For no man dies before his end. You don't know all that. What is dying then even? Nothing but the going silent of the caterpillar in the cocoon, which must tolerate it for the butterfly to be able to fly into the light. And the light, transfigured by me in the human, is a thousand times a thousand more glorious than the sun which stands over the earth."

The voice of death had changed entirely. He was speaking mildly and kindly and wisely, the way it existed behind the woman's deepest and most pious thoughts, though as a quite distant shimmer with which she was not familiar.

"Are you frightened of me still, Nagel?" death asked.

"Yes, death, I am still frightened. I beg, don't take it wrong. I am a woman, and my heart resists you", the Gotschdorf woman replied, and the tears ran over her cheeks at the same time. "You know I have lost two brothers, one in Galicia, one in France, and now the husband of my only sister has just fallen in Serbia. You may be right that dying is not so hard; but I am just poor Nagel from Gotschdorf, and by the coffin even the Countess at Warmbrunn is just a poor helpless woman. You, I beg you then imploringly for the sake of God, Maria and Christ, stop rampaging among us, for we humans, above all we women, can hardly bear in horror this worldwide slaying."

Death murmured something as if she could not understand.

"What do you mean?" Nagel asked.

But then she saw that death was seized again by pains.

"Woman", he cried fearfully, "woman! That is why I came to you. I cannot, I ..." Only, it was not possible for him to finish speaking. The attack seized and shook him again, and in the end, he emitted blood from his mouth like before, black, old blood, in clumps, and she saw that death was weak and dying.

When the struggle was over, he leant exhausted against the stone and let his head fall again.

Then Nagel stepped back again and thought it would be best that she went and let death die. Then the world would be rid of him and could breath out.

But she had hardly taken a step into the field margin when she heard him call weakly, "Come here, woman, quite close! Even if you run away, it will be no use to you humans. For if I die, you will have to suffer in life without end, and that is much worse than dying once. But dying! Oh God, dying! As long as there is life, the likes of us cannot go away, and life lasts eternally."

The woman thought of all the sorrows and all the worries, all the humiliations and all the destroyed hopes which she had suffered in her existence, and hesitated to leave.

Death felt how her heart was faltering in its depths and continued, "You did not let me finish speaking, woman. See, you humans have a horror of death. I have been seized by a horror of blood. I am sated, sated to the point of loathing. Even the sweetest, the most precious, the blood of youths is no longer to my taste. I long to go under the earth, to rest, for I am deathly faint with oversatiation. Help me, woman! Bury me and cover me up. I long for sleep. I want to lie for centuries and not wake anymore, for this meal of blood exceeds my powers, and yet I am death."

Nagel stood for a while and considered what she had heard. Then she made a quick turn and started running away.

"Why are you running away?" death called after her.

"I am going home and fetching a mattock and shovel", she called back over her shoulder.

"Stop, stay here!" death shouted. The order rang cutting like a knife so that she was frightened in her soul and could not go any further. Breathing heavily, she returned.

"Kneel here next to me", he said, "where I point to, there you are to scrape the earth away with your hands."

"I am not capable of that", Nagel responded. "The ground is frozen and I will hardly remove a crumb with my hands."

"Just attempt it", death said.

And the Gotschdorf woman did as she had been called. She bent down and grabbed at the earth. It was suddenly soft and loose as flour, and in a short time, she had finished a large grave, so deep that she could not see out.

"Now climb out and I will lie in it", death said.

With some effort, Nagel got out. Death climbed into the grave, set himself right with un-hurried satisfaction like an exhausted man and said with a contented smile, "Thank you, woman! Now I want to sleep, ah sleep, and the deeper I sink back into my heart, the more the slaying on earth will stop, until the people stand again in the doorways of their houses and die peacefully in my dreams which constantly pass over the earth. Thank you once more, woman! Go home in peace. You, your husband and your children, you are all safe from me until old age. Thank you! And now cover me with earth."

Nagel threw a few handfuls of earth on him. But then it occurred to her, if she buried death here in her fatherland, then he would awake in Germany too, and her grandchildren would then have to tolerate his horrors first. For that reason, she stopped again and stated her misgivings to death.

He blew the earth from his mouth and said, "Keep burying me in peace. I want to rest in German soil because I am safest among your people. They do not scare me and will only call for me in the most extreme need when the justice of God is violated on them. Then they shall quite safely wake me again with the sound of weapons, and I will ride amongst them in the war against their enemies. Meanwhile be kind to one another, for loveless men always wander through rubble even in peace. But now bury me and do not rest until you are finished."

The Gotschdorf woman took hold as if both her hands were shovels, and in a short time, the work was completed. At the end, she thought it would be better if she also rolled the boulders over death. The strength which she had received from the terrible one was still in her. She hardly needed to place her hands on the boulders and the stone gave way and sank over death deep into the ground. The lawn grew together around them, and soon after nobody could see what had occurred in this place.

When Nagel strode over the fields to the road, the thought came to her that she could have asked death for wealth and a new house. He who had all power over life would certainly have grudged her that. But straight after, it occurred to her that death offered only goods which would count for something in the eternity after this existence. She accepted that and continued on-ward.

At the main road, she was suddenly out of the circle of death and stood again in her old life. She did not know whether it had all really happened or had just been a vision.

But the longer pondered over it, the more joy-ful she became.

She returned to Gotschdorf, and to everyone who was amazed at her open eyes, she said that the terrible war would not last for a long time more, for death himself was sated with the blood of men. She betrayed to no one though, from whom she knew that.

***

I who have told this story have it from the little birch tree in the Gotschdorf field which saw everything. I stood one morning next to it, looked into the beautiful valley around me, as far as the wall of the Sudeten Mountains, and was at the sight of this peace sad over the laying waste and the rubble which this war has carried into so many lands, and over the hundreds of thousands of brothers who were drawn into the war never to be seen again. Then the little birch tree sud-denly gleamed in the reddish light of spring through its entire crown, and it entrusted me with the comforting story of the poor Gotschdorf woman.

The Fire Seeds

Until perhaps thirty or forty years ago, on the heights of the long slope which climbs up from the motley fields of the basin in which the prosperous village of Märzbach lies, a bleak dilapidated farmstead towered up which carried amongst the inhabitants of the surrounding area the name "the Frenchman's Fortress". Today you can only detect in the place, hidden under bushes and weeds, a few pitiful remnants of the walls.

Tied up with the puzzlingly quick decline of this once glorious property is the almost legendary history of the quick splendour and abrupt end of a family. A barrier of rocks through which a swiftly dropping narrow pass leads divides Märzbach's fertile expanse of fields from a sandy rolling plain on which the poor woodcutters' huts and weavers' cottages of Röderheide a strewn like a pack of hungry dogs.

From the little house of the weaver Frenzel, which bore its high jutting roof arduously close to the Royal Forest, a tall, pale youth stepped out in the memorable spring of the year 1812. The call "to my people" had penetrated as far as this distant corner of forest in Prussia. And the first of the district in which those tantalising words found an echo was Thaddäus Frenzel, the nineteen year old son of a father whom a long and futile struggle at the weaver's loom for the needs of daily life had crumpled and warped. The old man shuffled behind his son and escorted him to the little house's threshold. The sun was stretching its first rays like golden ladders up into the pale morning sky behind the Märzbach slope, and both sank for a while into the view of this great, heavenly auspice.

"The Märzbachers even get the sun first and the Röderers must chew on the salty crusts", the old weaver sighed, "but the misery grows quicker with us."

Thaddäus's look lay as if sucking on the first glow of light, and only a reluctant twitch of his shoulders betrayed that he had heard his father's words.

"Well, for my sake, always move and stir and twitch", the hunched man continued his last reminder fretfully, "what I have said, remains as it is. And don't think it brings luck to leave your parents. It would have to go funny in the world for the Lord to reveal golden thread exclusively to a weaver and sew silver buttons on his jacket. And in addition, with a jostling like war is. Indeed. The few grey hairs on my head will have been pulled out quickly enough by sorrow anyway with its little nippers; whether you stay here or not."

The anguish, almost as hot as hate, choked the old man, and he had to break off, for his breath was catching in his sunken chest.

Thaddäus now detached his eyes from the rapture and let them rest on the hunched, prematurely aged man with that deep, great light which with youth signifies: but I know better.

This silent arrogance irritated the mournful, despairing father quite properly.

"Leave off with that look! It is not as if I want to maintain that the Lord is, because of you, strewing golden wheat there over the Märzbach slope. Hey, is it not just the same when you yourself say all the time, I must, I must? Yes, boy, when you turn pale all of a sudden?"

Thaddäus was really shaken, not by the words of his father which he was long familiar with, but by the despairing gestures and the sobbing tone with which they had been spoken.

To get away from a hidden apprehensiveness, he turned his face again to the rising sun which was just then raising up the white fervour of its immediate vicinity behind the long slope. A reckless hope, which nevertheless lay indestructibly too deep within him, whispered to him a silent, defiant question: and why not? And the two stared as before wordlessly up into the pale blue heights.

Whilst they thus stood for a while, the legend tells, a glowing ball suddenly drew out of the depth of the heavens, came quickly nearer and burst over the Märzbach slope in countless glowing sparks which extinguished in falling like seeds of fire.

A cry of dismay arose from old Frenzel at this occurence which he held for a sign, and he crossed himself, trembling. Thaddäus, however, straightened up amidst heavy breaths, offered his father his hand and strode away from there deeply occupied.

Like a tall auspice for the realisation of his and his fatherland's fortunes, the pale, tall, weaver's son carried this chance event within himself, for the humiliations of outward poverty had not just pushed him from the low door of the paternal cottage, but he had also been touched by the holy clamour which had seized the German folk in that great year.

Those luminous sparks which had rained over him at his farewell to his home strengthened him in all the deprivations and lent him a stamina on onerous marches, a coldbloodedness in danger, a braveness in the attack which could not remain unnoticed. At Dennewitz, he stormed ahead to the ventursome mob who wrested the first cannons from the French. In Leipzig, he was among the reckless men who crept through the enemy and blew the Elster bridge up. At Bar-sur-Aube, he hewed apart a cuirassier bursting through who had already been swinging his sabre over Prince Wilhelm. Even before the confederated forces entered Paris, he received in recognition of his bravery an officer's commission and, after the short but murderish struggle of a hundred days, was released from service richly endowed.

When he returned to Röderheide in autumn of the year 1817, he found his parents dead, buried under sunken, overgrown burial mounds, his parents' house occupied by strangers and his siblings scattered. Although he could not, because of his stubbornness, act in his heart unjustly, his inwardly turned mood was beset by a painful darkening when he heard under what circumstances his father had died. Already a year after his escape from his parents' house, the ailing man had been beset by a creeping fever, that consequence of lifelong hunger and constant worry which, a slow, fervent withering, hollowed him out inwardly. Soon he lay powerless, staring with desperate eyes, in the bed which he had to have placed by that window from which he could look at the Märzbach slope. In more propitious moments of the illness, he straightened up arduously and looked raptly and wordlessly over it. The mother however, driven by a mad turmoil of anguish into despair, also left her place at the loom and ran from house to house, from farm to farm. She seemed to have lost her mind and roamed about all day begging, returning haggardly in the evening mostly with empty hands and sinking down powerlessly by the invalid's bed amidst quiet tears. There she spent the entire night, sleeping on the floor. But in the morning she again started that mad wandering, seeking help. Thus it went for weeks. Then neighbours saw one day very early, not long after the departure of the madly sorrowful woman, the door to the weaver's cottage hesitantly open and the invalid come crawling on hands and knees over the threshold. He was only dressed in a shirt and, when he had happily escaped his house, he lifted his emaciated hands as if imploring and beseeching towards the sun hovering in rapt brightness over the slope of Märzbach. Before the people could rush to help, he collapsed and was carried dying to his bed. When his wife came home and saw that her husband was dead, she instantly stopped crying, brushed her hair back, dressed in her Sunday best as if she wanted to go away with him anew, and laid herself down by the lifeless man. In that same night, she also passed away.

Thaddäus Frenzel listened to the tale of his parent's end, and as befit a man who has come so close to death so often, his face barely stirred. Only with the mention of the hardheartedness of the farmers did an angry smile play about his mouth. He comported himself over winter calmly in the small room of the tavern which he had rented. Towards spring, he settled on the quiet the purchase of one of the largest farms in Märzbach, whose broad fields stretched over the heights of the slope, and counted out the entire sum in cash. In May of the same year, he began the building of the farmstead in the place over which the mysterious ball of fire had once splattered in glittering seeds. The old buildings in the village, however, were demolished. If the envy at the news of the purchase of the large estate in Märzbach and Röderheide had been vented in all sorts of speculations over the acquisition of his wealth, then the suspicions were enlarged into adventurous rumours when Thaddäus Frenzel, the weaver's son, had a farmstead erected on the heights, which left behind in the vast extent and peculiarity of its conception everything which was customary in that district. — Lusty as reeds, as it were overnight, the building shot up, and while the people were still sharpening their mouths for mockery of the expected follies, the walls rose up all around to the roof. The traditional idleness of the workers was transformed under the calm, unrelenting eyes of Frenzel into feverish activity, and to some under the walls itself, it seemed indubitable that the building was not raised by natural powers. If you did not see the Frenchman Frenzel, after the builders had long scattered down to Märzbach or Röderheide, daily, often until the stars appeared in the heavens, sitting on the wall in silent rapture or striding excitedly back and forth as if an evil spirit were chasing him, or when he, not just once, stood on the highest pinnacle of his building, hard by the edge, in such a daringly wild pose, then it was no wonder if the superstitious farmers ensnared themselves more and more stubbornly in the belief that Thaddäus had signed a pact with the devil. After this word had first dropped, the building was, in the eyes of the surrounding residents, enlivened with all sorts of monstrosities. Hellish spirits were seen in the mists of moonlit nights billowing about the walls, the whining or laughing of eternal madness was heard through the wailing of the wind, and the sleepless old men sometimes heard in the darkness a creaking wagon, cracking whips and grisly oaths travelling high through the air. Nobody doubted it now anymore either, that Frenzel had robbed the money pouches of the fallen on the battlefield and had cut fingers from the hands of the dead to glean their rings. In this way, the mysteriously inexhaustible wealth was explained which Thaddäus Frenzel seemed to have at his disposal.

When the first leaves of the lime trees began to discolour, the rooflayer was caulking the last tabs on the roofridge of the farmstead. Battlemented like a castle, the building lay four storeys high. The residence strove up massively like a tower over the farm buildings. A sinister prying peered from its windows. The antiquated outgrowths looked like mad exuberance.

People were outraged most of all over mysterious symbols which were inset in a sort of escutcheon over the keystone of the archway, over the front door, and recurring high on the gable. On a skyblue ground, three golden balls floated. At that time, nobody yet knew the actual significance of this image, and it was explained simply as the emblem of the devil's order of freemasons. In this way, the circle was closed in the souls of the farmers. The incomprehensible rise of the weaver's son and his so entirely differently mannered being were no longer recognised as the defiant straying of a human life which someday, purified by blows or misfortune, could be put back on the path of others, but rather he had been caught from the start in the machinations of evil forces. The initial, passionate outrage of the people hence changed suddenly into a contempt muffled by fear and dread to the point of gestures of ingratiating goodwill.

Thaddäus, for whom the fire seeds did not merely hover over the entrance way and the gable, and whose will was constantly held in high tension by a distant gleaming, hardly noticed any of the change in his surroundings or, as a lowly-born and battle-hardened man who had learnt to despise both the masks of the day and the grimaces of the crowd, gave little attention to the sneaking secret malice and consoled himself probably that the house was nothing but a bell with which sometimes battle, sometimes peace could be tolled. He filled the sheds with the necessary farm equipment, the stalls with cattle, and settled in the highest room of his residence under the roof amidst sparse comforts. Thus he lived withdrawn for a few years, devoted only to breaking himself in to the unaccustomed occupation, and harvested the delight that his industry, his stamina, and not the least his thrusting mind accounted for unforthcoming mistakes, increased his prosperity, and safeguarded his confidence in his powers.

He remained alone for five years. Then he noticed that a farm without a farmwife is a body without legs, and attempted, in order to find a wife, to establish relations with the landowners of his village and the surrounds. He encountered everywhere steely reticence, restained contempt or open rejection. Without further ado, he made his maid his farmwife, a black-haired, joyful being who was anaemic and pretty as a picture. As little as her open, quite meddlesome manner appeared to agree with his taciturn, preoccupied disposition, he took the girl to his bed.

Already in the first year, she bore him a son and heir whom he gave the name of his father Franziskus.

After that gratifying event, the ruthless tension of his powers loosened a little in the taciturn man. Without suffering any loss of his decisiveness in the least, a gentle lounging back into a serene shimmer came over him, a shimmer which had blossomed into a patient, quiet expectation hidden in his soul. There were moments when he leant over the little one's cradle or strode alone in the fields in spring, in which all that was harsh in his face dissolved into a sunny radiance. If his life withdrew into itself as before, and he also did not induct his wife into the concealments of his soul, she seemed not to go without anything, and this quite distant kindness obviously grieved her little. Her unrelenting industry took hold everywhere, nothing escaped her lively black eyes. Although that same passionate joyfulness adorned her as before, she knew to preserve the appropriate distance towards the servants. The two labourers especially, she governed with a look. For she did not spare herself and did not know in particular the darkness of what was coming up. Yes, in her courageous work, she sometimes did too much and took hold of activities which were actually only matters for men. Once Thaddäus even noticed out his window how, far out in the fields, she wrested the plough from a young labourer against his protests and then steered the iron through the field confidently and immaculately.

The farmer thought of this incident one Sunday afternoon when, reclining in his comfortable chair, he looked at the smoke from his pipe in all kinds of hopes which reached out from his colourful, multifaceted past and played out as dreamily beautiful accomplishments in the distant future. The windows stood open. From the stalls, the clattering chains of the cows rang out and the dull stamping of the horses. His wife was rocking the child ever more gently over by the wall next to the stove. Then the cradle fell silent, and she also sat, her hands folded in her lap, and looked raptly out into the Sunday-still yard. The labourer whom she had once wrested the plough from in the fields was passing through with revelling step, tarried for a moment in the room, whistled the beginning of a song and then strode down the hall and up the stairs.

After a few moments, his wife also rose. He heard her in the adjoining room opening and closing drawers, rattling in the glass cabinet amongst the cups, and finally she vanished out the back door. Now it was so quiet in the large, high-ceilinged room that Thaddäus could hear flies knocking against the windowpanes. The unhurried tailing off into thousands of images surged more and more shadowlike within him, and to fend off falling asleep, but still caught in dream, he rose and walked about, so as to not entirely break those blissful shadows, with quiet, long strides. No will, no intention led him. Thus he made it across the hall, up the stairs, and found himself, not unlike a sleepwalker, suddenly in the loft of the house in darkness. Then he came to his senses with a gentle shock and, smiling to himself, passed his right hand over his forehead. With rooms to the left and right, the narrow corridor opened further on into a large loft room from whose depths strips of light flashed from little dormer windows.

On the point of turning his feet and returning, he heard somewhere the voice of his young wife speaking in a whisper and hotly imploring amidst the ardent murmur of a man. An painful bronze hand grasped his heart. On trembling legs, he shuffled forwards. But, after how many steps, he did not know, it suddenly seemed to him as if all the air around him was whinnying like a horse going wild, and a dull crashing took hold over him. Thus the fury sprang up in him. With a leap, he was at the door to the room, tore the labourer up from a whirl of sparks, lifted him up and smashed him wordlessly on the ground next to him. And as the culprit lay still and bleeding before him, a rigid, pale light fell on his wife, cowering in randy nakedness on the bed, her head lowered, whimpering, and shaken all over by the shivering of remorse and shame. At the sight of her, a sobbing force began to work in the chest of the betrayed farmer, almost a sort of pity. But only for the length of a breath did this sinking back tremble through him, then he stepped up to her with his cold step as she fell against the wall, in expectation of the terrible thing which must now befall her, and waited with pale face and eyes wide-open in fear of her punishment. Only Frenzel took the clothes from her clutching hand, spat in the middle of her beautiful, desperate eyes, then left the room and carefully locked the door behind him. — At the same time, he strode erectly across the visibly lifeless labourer and down into his room.

In the middle of the night, he fetched the adulteress from her confinement and drove her with lashes of a whip from the farm. He had left her nothing but her shirt and her child. Breathless with fury, he finally stood still and let the whimpering fugitive disappear like a pale ghost into the darkness.

Then he returned, locked the yard gate and threw the keys over the walls out into the field. Since that day, he never left the farmstead again. Already after a few years, birch trees were nestling in the cracking walls. The panes of the windows smashed. The roof was holed by storms. Doors and the gate fell from their hinges. Around the yard, an oppressive smell of decay lay as if it were a single rotting corpse. Thaddäus Frenzel sat in the topmost room, in that room which he had resided in before marrying, surrounded by the meagre comforts of his great hope, and stared unmoving over the Märzbach basin at that corner of forest in Röderheide where the cottage of his father still stood, now as if in happy, wishless poverty. —

It may have lasted twenty years. On one of those November nights when the Lord strews shooting stars like a sparkling seed through the heavens, the unfortunate man clambered to a window and plunged down onto the heap of stones on the steep slope.

Even today the people of Märzbach point to the spot on which this long-hated man came crashing to his death. Little flowers whose delicate stems shake in the lightest of breezes cover the stones with their mildewy-green leaves and bear countless flaming dark star-like flowers. People say they grew from the blood of the suicide, and nobody dares to break one off, so as to preserve themselves from misfortune.

Thus the portal to the memory of this poor man is still today the fire seeds which once raised his life so high and plunged it so deep.

About the Publisher

Our mission is to provide translations into English of the complete works of neglected major European writers. We do not cherry-pick works that seem the most marketable, but rather seek to provide a complete collection of each writer's works so that readers can follow the writer's development and decide on its merits for themselves.

http://www.facebook.com/KANitzPublishing